MISTRESS OF SINS

DREDTHORNE HALL BOOK 3

HAZEL HUNTER

Hazel loves hearing from readers!
You can contact her at the links below.

Website: hazelhunter.com

Facebook:
business.facebook.com/HazelHunterAuthor

Newsletter: HazelHunter.com/news

I send newsletters with details on new releases, special offers, and other bits of news related to my writing. You can sign up here!

CHAPTER 1

A familiar shriek from outside the sitting room made Jennet Reed set down her tea cup and watch the door, resigned to the knowledge that it would soon fling open. Outside the window providing pale sunlight for her morning tea, curls of dying leaves drifted past on a brisk October breeze. All around Reed Park the gardeners would spend the day clearing out the last of the sparse garden beds and gather bulbs for winter storage. Since rising early usually allowed Jennet to enjoy her cozy spot alone for the first hours of the day, she felt rather annoyed.

Rapid footsteps followed the cry, and then Margaret Reed entered with the speed of a woman being hounded by an angry mob. Short, plump and swaddled in a pink velvet dressing gown, she clutched a crumpled paper, which she waved like a flag of frantic surrender.

"Oh, Jennet, oh my dear." Her mother's loose silver-blonde ringlets bobbed wildly around her pale face as she hurried over to the settee, enveloping it with her violet scent. "I found the most detestable missive in amongst the notes and cards that came yesterday. We will be cursed."

"Again?" Jennet drew Margaret down beside her and took the note from her trembling hands. She read over the brief, unsigned message before she looked into her mother's terrified pale blue eyes. "Mama, this is an invitation. Someone wishes me to attend an All Hallows' Eve masquerade at Dredthorne Hall."

"It says that a curse will be cast over us." Her mother stabbed a finger at the paper. "Unless you go to that monstrous place on that evil night, where I am sure you will be murdered, and I left to die in my old age, bereft and alone."

"Nonsense." That pronouncement

caused Margaret to burst into tears. Jennet sighed and searched for her handkerchief.

Allowing her mother to weep for a few moments seemed judicious; Margaret had always been highly-strung and easily distressed, and after an uneventful month likely needed the respite. Once Jennet heard the first hiccup of abating sobs she gently mopped up her mother's tears and made her a cup of too-sweet tea. Then she tackled the contents of the note.

"No one wishes us ill, Mama," she assured Margaret. "Curses are not real, you know this. Mr. Branwen explained that to you in great detail when we broached the subject with him."

"What could a vicar know of the misery that haunts our name?" her mother demanded, wringing the now-damp handkerchief. "Has all of his family died while still young? Did he lose his dear Papa even before he was born? Was he abandoned at the altar on his wedding day?"

And there, Jennet thought, was the story of her life in just three questions. Aside from her and her widowed mother, all of their family had died, most of them in their prime. Margaret never cared to be reminded of the reckless, stubborn streak every Reed possessed along with the family's auburn tresses and green eyes. That tempestuous flaw had contributed to those early demises, including her father's. He'd gone off to die fighting the French only a few months after marrying and impregnating Margaret.

Eighteen years later…

No. Jennet would not think about the most ridiculous chapter in her own rather dull saga. She had sworn never to waste another moment thinking about that bounder, that scoundrel, that deceitful, heartless beast of a man.

"Mama," she said, using a firm tone she usually reserved for cheeky footmen and over-curious villagers, "We are not being cursed. I daresay it is a joke in poor taste, nothing more."

"Who would do such a monstrous thing?" Margaret demanded.

"Someone who wishes me to attend so that I might amuse their guests." Jennet already suspected just who that might be. "I imagine they wished to make the invitation seem appropriate to the occasion."

"By cursing us?" her mother shrieked, and then pressed her hand to her brow. "Oh, this will end me now, surely. My head pounds with such violence. Where is Debny? She must send for Dr. Mallory before it is too late."

Since they had reached the second act in Margaret's hysterics, Jennet eyed the door again. Her mother's lady's maid came in a moment later, as Debny knew to wait in the hall until she heard her name uttered. With the skill of much practice she coaxed Margaret upstairs to her bed chamber. Her assurances of a soothing tisane, a headache powder and a summons for the village doctor did much more than Jennet could to calm her mistress. Their housekeeper then came in to apologize for leaving the post unattended; she had been in the kitchen going over the week's menus with their cook.

"Do not blame yourself, Mrs. Holloway," Jennet said as she folded the invitation and tucked it in her reticule. "Mama hasn't been distressed for at least a fortnight, so she sought an excuse. Do ask Cook to prepare some light broth for her luncheon, and keep the herbals brewing until the doctor arrives."

The housekeeper nodded as she handed over the rest of the post. "I beg your pardon, Miss, but the butcher's lad mentioned that the Tindalls returned from London yesterday."

"That is welcome news." And a chance to escape her mother's latest bout of agitation, Jennet thought as she rose from the settee. "Please have Barton ready the rig."

AFTER LOOKING in on her mother, Jennet changed from her morning muslin to a dark green walking dress, and donned a brown hooded wool cloak. While not as fashionable as a spencer jacket, the cloak would keep her warm on the chilly drive over to Tindall House.

She did not care to brood over her appearance greatly. With such prominent cheekbones, full lips and a faintly cleft chin she would always be called handsome rather than pretty, but she preferred that. Youthful beauty faded; a good bone structure lasted forever.

Her hair she braided and coiled to keep it tidy during the drive. The thick mass of it had grown quite long over the summer, and soon she would have to trim it to a more manageable length. Thus far she had not found any gray hairs to pluck away, but she suspected she would go the way of the Reed side of the family. Legend had it that their dark red hair never silvered, but only paled to coppery-gold with age—if any of them had truly lived so long.

Such vanity, Jennet thought as she turned away from the looking glass. *Who will care what color your hair turns?*

Margaret would scold her for dressing as well as driving herself, but Jennet preferred self-reliance over playing the genteel lady. Besides being cursed and jilted at the altar, she had now reached a definite spinster's age of seven and twenty. Certain privileges did come along with the disadvantages.

Barton, who managed the stables as well

as the deliveries, waited outside the house with the prepared rig.

"Morning, Miss." He tugged at the brim of his hat before he helped Jennet up into the driver's seat and handed her the reins. "Mrs. H. said we're to expect Dr. Mallory?"

"Yes, for Mama." She exchanged a knowing look with him; all of the servants were well-acquainted with Margaret's frequent panics. "Nothing serious, but please do watch for him. I will return by luncheon."

Barton nodded. "Very good, Miss."

Going to the Tindall estate gave Jennet time to enjoy the palette of autumn, which had painted most of Renwick in myriad fiery colors. The fields remained green, and patches of white and purple heather daubed the hillsides, but the trees had gone crimson, gold and apricot. Some of the largest oaks and ashes looked as if countless tiny flames blazed from their branches. Despite the damp chill of the morning air, Jennet preferred this time of year to any other in the countryside. Summer's bounty had been harvested, and the snows had yet to arrive. It seemed the perfect season.

That was why you chose to marry in October, so the church could be adorned in autumnal splendor, to match your garnet hair and witch's eyes.

"I did not marry," Jennet told the errant thought as she guided the horse up the winding drive to her friend's home. "I am not a witch."

You bewitch me, a deep voice chided from her memory.

Once more Jennet saw herself in her wedding gown, standing in the church while a younger Mr. Branwen comforted a noisily weeping Margaret, and hundreds of guests whispered and stared at her. She had been like a pillar of salt, frozen for all eternity halfway to an empty altar where her marriage would not be taking place. Later she would feel the humiliation, the despair, and the deep and abiding hatred of the man who had so thoroughly ruined her. In that moment, however, all she could think was how even with her gift she had never anticipated this, not once. She believed she had been loved as much as she had loved.

Never again.

Although it was a little early for a morning call, the Tindalls' butler welcomed Jennet with a smile. "Miss Catherine is in the library, Miss Reed."

As she made her way through the house Jennet noted the finest of the latest décor fashions had accompanied the family from London, including new opulent gold-trimmed draperies and exotic-looking chairs with curved legs and inlays of brass. The Tindall family had no qualms about displaying their taste for the modern, or the affluence that allowed them to indulge it.

In the library she found Catherine dozing on an ebonized chaise of green damask, her lemon silk morning gown making her appear as if wrapped in a beam of early sunlight. Artful curls of brown escaped her sophisticated, golden-laced Greco-Roman hairstyle to frame her rose-cheeked face. Against her breast lay an open volume of Shakespeare's sonnets, adding a romantic note to the tableau.

"What do I look like?" Catherine asked without opening her eyes. "A pretty demure miss, or an enchanting, provocative coquette?"

"You are everything without artifice," Jennet assured her drily. "Except for the Shakespeare. Everyone knows how you hate to read."

"Sadly, true." Her friend wrinkled her nose, tossed the book aside and sat up to grin at her. "So, you must amuse me now that I am whisked from the diversions of London. I have news, but you must first tell me that you have an intrigue to share. I dare not hope for a scandal in Renwick."

Extracting the bedraggled note from her reticule, she offered it to Catherine. "An All Hallows' Eve masquerade at Dredthorne may suffice."

"Egad. I received one of these, too. A masked ball at the most haunted mansion in the county seems rather ghastly. I can hardly contain my excitement." Her friend read the invitation and chuckled. "I imagine you know why you were singled out."

Jennet sighed and nodded as she sat down on a chintz-covered chair across from Catherine. Since childhood she had possessed a natural talent for deciphering the feelings and intentions of others. Although she herself didn't know how, she could always tell what most people were thinking by the changes in their reactions, expressions and stances during conversation. This gift allowed her to anticipate and avoid a great deal of that which she regarded as unpleasant, but it had also given her a reputation as a natural diviner.

"In London the new fashion in fortune-telling is to gaze into a crystal ball while making predictions," Catherine told her as she turned the note over. "Mine was also unsigned. Who do you think sent them?"

"Mr. Pickering, I daresay." Jennet tugged off her gloves. "He's called three times since he came back from the city, and told Mama he has leased a property near Reed Park for a shooting party."

"Ah, the ever-determined Arthur. I quite forgot his fascination with you." Her friend sighed. "He is not titled, handsome or particularly interesting, and I must say his dancing is entirely dreadful. Still, you could do worse."

"I thank you for your opinions." Her enthusiasm for London society meant Catherine knew everything about everyone, which sometimes proved annoying. "As I have told Mr. Pickering many times, I have no intention of marrying."

"Even when the gentleman has a house in Grosvenor's Square, and seven thousand a year?" Her friend grinned as she handed back the invitation. "I am certain that he has mentioned that on a dozen occasions."

"I am not concerned with Mr. Pickering," Jennet told her crisply. "Mama found the invitation first, and you know how nonsensical she becomes about curses. I think I must attend, if only to prove to her that nothing dreadful will happen. Yet she will not allow me to go to Dredthorne Hall alone, for fear of the ghosts she believes haunts it."

"A frightful dilemma." Catherine gave her a wry look. "You may tell dear Mrs. Reed that we will attend the masquerade together. I will play bodyguard and not for a moment leave your side."

"The ball will be held in three days," she pointed out, "and we have no costumes."

"We can make our own masks." Her friend rose from the chaise. "My grandmother's trunks should contain something suitably decrepit to serve as our regalia. Come, we must raid the attics."

A short time later they came downstairs with two old but still-wearable ball gowns, which Catherine gave to her maid to clean and press. She then retrieved two lengths of velvet, matching ribbon and the sewing box from her room so they could fashion masks.

"A domino style is simple to sew, and will provide adequate concealment," Catherine said as they went back to the library. "Although to keep our identities entirely concealed we should powder our hair, or perhaps wear wigs."

"I should first shave my head bare," Jennet said, only half in jest.

Her friend laughed. "Now that would discourage Mr. Pickering."

As they sewed, Catherine chattered on about the many exciting parties and balls she had attended in London. Jennet felt a rare twinge of envy, for she had nothing similar to confide. Society in Renwick could only be regarded as staid and unvarying, with the occasional assembly or country dance, and she hardly bothered to attend half of those.

She didn't mind their neighbors, or the simple pleasures they enjoyed together. Their efforts to include her, however, came more from compassion than any desire for her company. Jennet in turn had a reputation for always leaving early, but not because she quickly wearied of Renwick society. At such events she often overheard murmured remarks that illustrated the general sympathy directed toward her.

Luckless girl. I think she will never recover from being so meanly treated.

As handsome as she ever was, but far too old now to attract another offer.

At least she can be a comfort to her mother.

To keep her temper in check in those moments Jennet would then have to claim fatigue to her host and leave. She quite despised being made forever the object of pity, especially when she felt quite the opposite. How fortunate she had been, to be spared marriage to a man so unfeeling he had not even bothered to call off their wedding. No, he had run off to London, the coward, without a word to anyone. His own parents had been so ashamed by his betrayal they had packed up and left Renwick at once, and since had only rarely visited their country house.

Of what had happened immediately after she had been jilted Jennet remembered very little. She knew she must have come home with her mother, and walked upstairs to her chamber to change. When the room grew dark, she supposed she had slept; she had no recollection of any of it. Her first clear memory was standing over the torn ruin of her wedding gown, and then politely asking Mrs. Holloway to burn the shredded heap rather than use it as rags.

"Only if you'll eat something, Miss," the housekeeper said firmly, nodding toward the untouched tray by her bed.

"Of course." Jennet wanted nothing but to crawl back into her bed, but starving herself to death for him seemed worse than being left at the altar. "Do forgive me."

Seven years had passed since her jilting, years that had bestowed on her the grace of acceptance. That she had never shed a single tear, nor allowed the disgrace to rule the rest of her life, provided Jennet with great solace. She remained as she ever had been, only perhaps a little wiser about men and matters of the heart.

"Once my maid adds a bit of lace and beading, this should do," Catherine said, drawing Jennet out of her thoughts. She tied on the black mask she had sewn, tucked a hand under her chin, and pursed her lips. "Do I appear mysterious?"

"Utterly." Jennet pinned the ribbons to either side of her blue velvet domino. "I think I will embroider mine with some silks I have at home. I should go."

"You cannot leave yet. All our talk of Mr. Pickering made me forget the most important news." Her friend removed the mask and set it aside as she gave her a sly look. "It seems our old friend William Gerard has come back to Renwick. Do you think he will attend the masquerade?"

"I cannot tell you," Jennet said, keeping her expression bland. "Why would it matter?"

"You have not heard." Catherine's voice dropped to a confidential murmur.

"William's father died last year from lung fever, poor gentleman, so he is Baron Greystone now." She sighed. "Every scheming mama with an unattached daughter will be calling at Gerard Lodge. Still, Papa said he arrived only yesterday, so I think he will be too busy settling in to make an appearance."

"I expect he will." Jennet knew nothing would hinder the competition for Greystone's attention; marriageable men of suitable fortune did not often take up residence in Renwick. What he had done before inheriting the barony mattered little.

Her friend peered at her. "I had expected you would have much to say on the matter."

Jennet's hand shook, driving the sharp end of her needle into her fingertip. The pain provided the immediate return of her customary clarity. "Was that your motive for telling me of his lordship's return?"

"I truly meant only to tease you," her friend said, grimacing. "I should have thought better of it. When the Duke of Bedford refused to dance with me during my first season, I thought it should break my heart. Papa so wished for me to become engaged to him."

Although she had received innumerable offers, Catherine remained unmarried, which had always puzzled Jennet. "Surely there have been others who might please your father."

"Those who have satisfied him were gentlemen I found very disagreeable, and those I have favored he disdained." She shrugged. "Truly, I rather like my situation. I am invited to all the balls and gatherings. I can travel where I like, and see my friends whenever I choose. I will inherit all this someday. Why marry at all?"

Jennet tucked her needle into the velvet, and rubbed her throbbing finger against her palm. "You do not yearn for love, or children?"

"I know too much about men to fall in love," Catherine said. "Child-bearing seems a vastly dreary business." Her nose wrinkled. "I consider myself blessed whenever I see Bedford now. The years since have stolen most of His Grace's hair, and bestowed on him the look of a petulant dormouse."

"Yet he would have made you a Duchess, my dear," Eleanor Tindall said as she came into the library. As petite as her daughter, the lady wore a sumptuous gown of dark blue velvet with gleaming insets of golden brocade. "Good afternoon, dear Jennet. I hope you will stay for luncheon."

"Thank you, ma'am, but I think I must go home." Jennet tucked her mask into her reticule. "Thank you for helping me to avert all possible disaster, Catherine. I will call for you on the night of the masquerade at dusk."

"I will have the gown sent to Reed Park tomorrow," her friend said as she walked with her to the front entry. When Jennet murmured her thanks and kissed her cheek Catherine took hold of her hands. "Do not permit the specter of the past to spoil our fun. What is in the past is dead. He is nothing to you now."

"You are quite right." She forced a smile and then went to the rig.

On the drive back to Reed Park Jennet reined in the horse at a crossing, and then turned onto another, seldom-used road that led in the opposite direction. Soon she crossed fresh wheel ruts left by the recent passage of heavily-laden carts, and passed a meadow of withering grasses glinting with drops of melting frost.

The afternoon sun felt hot on the back of her neck as she approached another turn, this one onto a drive leading up to an imposing country manor. The house, clad in dark stone and roofed in charcoal slate, had double-hung sash windows and a fan panel over the front door, in which had been placed panes of black and white glass cut and fitted to resemble a crescent moon in a star-studded night sky. White stone and severely-trimmed evergreens hemmed the outer walls, and flanked the stone carriage house to one side.

He had hated the house, Jennet recalled, and yet it remained unchanged.

The lodge is a nightmare to the eye. When my father dies I will paint it apricot and scarlet, and have the gardeners fill the lawns with daisies and dandelions. Then you may make a wish each time you walk outside, while I fashion flower crowns for you to wear every day.

How many such fanciful notions had they shared during their engagement? For a moment Jennet felt the pain of her loss again, as if the man she had adored had died rather than deserted her. This was to have been her home, their home, which he had promised they would fill with laughter and children. Margaret would have come often to visit her grandchildren. They would have had their friends over for dinners and parties and holiday gatherings, and watched their sons and daughters grow, and lived the life of anyone's dreams.

"You fool," Jennet whispered as she stared at Gerard Lodge. Whether she addressed its master or herself, she could not say.

As she tugged on the reins to turn the rig around, Jennet felt hollow yet resolute. Should Baron Greystone choose to attend the masquerade, like the other guests he would be in costume. That would likely avert any possibility of an unhappy encounter. She could enjoy the evening with Catherine and their friends without worry.

And if Greystone dared to remove his mask, why then, she would simply punch her former fiancé in the face.

CHAPTER 2

*O*utside the parsonage, Jeffrey Branwen surveyed the flower garden with the resignation of a man who had witnessed many such disappointments. His shadow, shorter and rounder than himself, stretched out before him like a puddle of a mourning gown—or a gigantic black thumb. Out of habit he rubbed the back of his neck as he tried to fathom where he had gone wrong with this effort.

In every way, he thought, for his garden had withered entirely. One would find more flowers blooming in a graveyard.

The roses he had tried to coax into bloom had all died during the late summer without offering so much as a single bud. The violets, so adored by his wife Deidre, had accompanied them into the great garden beyond. So had the lavender, the morning glories, and the poppies. A few weeds had poked up when he had admitted defeat at the beginning of fall, but they, too, now browned and drooped. He also suspected the young elm sapling he had installed by Deidre's bench to provide shade had grown diseased.

He would not think about the vegetable patch, which had fallen victim to slugs so voracious they had all but cleared the ground for him.

"What are you doing out here in all this wind, sir?" a sweet voice called.

Jeffrey turned his head to see his wife coming from the house with his cloak in her arms. "Mourning the departed, my love. I am sorry to say that the last of the roses has sought eternal rest."

"Ah, well, they will be in good company." Deidre pulled the heavy wool over his shoulders before she regarded the dead plants. "I am sure they were sorry to leave us. They always are, you know."

"I am happy it amuses you." He kissed the tip of her nose. "Really, I am an

Englishman. We are a nation of gardeners. Why can I grow nothing more than sticks?"

"Perhaps you were meant to be a cane weaver." She tucked her arms around his waist. "Or a school master."

Jeffrey narrowed his eyes. "Stop laughing at me." He glanced down and saw a note in her hand. "Has someone need of their vicar? For I cannot recommend myself as a gardener."

"It is an invitation." The smile fled from her pretty face. "We are invited to a masquerade at Dredthorne Hall. There is no signature, but Lady Hardiwick mentioned to me that Mr. Arthur Pickering has leased the property." She held out the folded paper.

Jeffrey's first instinct was to tear up the invitation and toss the pieces into the compost barrel. Instead he took it and tucked it into his jacket. "Is there some tea left from breakfast? I am in need of a cup."

Deidre nodded, and accompanied him into the parsonage, where she prepared a tray and brought it to their sitting room.

Jeffrey inspected the large pile of

biscuits she had brought with the pot and their cups. "Ginger nuts?"

"The Sisters Brexley sent a tin for you. They are very good for the digestion," his wife said as she poured and handed him his tea. "Especially as I did not bake them. That invitation is not going to set well, so do have some. It is too early in the day for brandy."

"We never drink spirits," he reminded her.

"If I am to go to that abominable house in a costume and dance, I may begin." Deidre saw his expression and sighed. "Oh, dearest, must we go?"

Being the vicar of Renwick was more than Jeffrey's position or calling; he had a spiritual obligation to his parish. As the representative of the church, he regarded his duty as more than simply holding services on Sunday or visiting the sick and elderly. By attending the various gatherings and assemblies he provided a wholesome presence. Often just the sight of him would calm the over-boisterous and discourage the sinful.

The fact that they had been invited to a

masquerade did not trouble him; the location did.

Dredthorne Hall had changed hands several times over the last years. Built more than a century past by an affluent merchant name Emerson Thorne, who admired all things French, it had been designed to imitate one of the great chateaus in that country. Enormous, imposing and surrounded by a large estate, the hall had once been regarded as one of the most impressive buildings in England. Then terrible events began to take their toll on Thorne; his wife had suddenly died and he had become a recluse. His descendants had fared little better, and rumors of a family curse began to circulate widely. Soon no one wanted to go near the great house or have anything to do with the Thornes.

Jeffrey did not believe in curses, but he knew from tragic personal experience that Dredthorne Hall seemed to attract evil as surely as a tavern drew drunkards.

At present the house was owned by a property concern that owned many estates north of London, which had been leasing it for hunting parties and private events. The rates, considered cheap by city standards, often lured bachelors to bring their friends to Dredthorne for hunting and shooting. Arthur Pickering's choice to hold a costume ball there should not have seemed odd, but it did.

"Mr. Pickering seems a very mannerly gentleman," Deidre said, in the way she had when Jeffrey had gone silent for too long. "I quite liked making his acquaintance when he came to church. I am sure he would not mind if we refused his invitation. A ball held on All Hallows' Eve is not in keeping with the church's views."

He took a nibble from a ginger nut. "You believe we should refuse him."

"I believe I should trust your judgment, as ever I do." She put down the biscuit. "There will be no reminders of what your sister endured there. It was so long ago that everyone but you and I have forgotten."

Jeffrey would never forget learning that his sister Lucetta had been shot by a madman in Dredthorne Hall's front foyer, or that she had come close to bleeding to death and dying there. He hated the reminder of how hopeless and helpless he had felt as he had waited to learn from the doctor if she would survive. He recalled every day she had spent with him and Deidre at the parsonage, slowly recovering from the savage wound. The ending to that story could only be called joyful, but he would never feel the same about the ordeal.

Many of his young parishioners would go to the ball. Someone had to look out for them.

"I think we must attend," he told his wife. "We need not stay very long, but I wish to make an appearance."

Deidre didn't look happy, but she nodded and held out a ginger nut for him. "We will want costumes to wear, unless you wanted to play the vicar and his wife."

He thought for a moment. "Perhaps we might employ some metaphor in that."

CHAPTER 3

The next day Jennet made sure her mother was sleeping before she set out for the village from Reed Park. Dr. Mallory had stopped in and prescribed rest and an herbal soother for Margaret, and checked with the housekeeper to insure they had some laudanum on hand if her panic escalated.

"I should think she will recover in a day or so, Miss Reed," the doctor advised her before leaving to attend his next patient. "Until she does, keep her indoors and well-wrapped against chill, and avoid provoking excitement."

Debny promised to sit with Margaret while Jennet attended to her errands, which included a stop at the haberdasher's shop.

She hoped to find embroidery threads to match the old gown Catherine had lent her, but as soon as she entered the establishment she saw a clutch of young ladies giggling over the fine laces.

The proprietor greeted her with a ready smile. "Good afternoon, Miss Reed. May I be of service?"

"I think I will browse, sir," she told him, and went over to the threads cabinet, where she pulled out the drawer for shades of blue. She had clipped a tiny piece of the gown's silk from an inner seam, and took it from her reticule to compare it to the available stock.

"I hear he is very tall, and dark, and has the broadest shoulders," one of the girls at the laces counter said, cooing the words. "Perhaps he will dress as Wellington, and carry a sword."

"Surely not, for I have seen the Iron Duke, and he is nothing at all," another claimed. "He is very short and slight, and has a hooked nose." She drew an outline of the latter over her own.

"I think he should dress as Mr. Brummel, for I daresay he is just as elegant, and a hundred times as rich," a third girl put in, making all of them giggle at her shocking remark. "And I will dress as the Queen of France, so he will not be able to resist asking me to dance."

"Rose Abernathy, you are utterly shameless," the first girl accused.

"Why? Because I wish to make the acquaintance of a rich, unattached gentleman with a title, who may desire a wife?" Rose made a contemptuous sound. "It is not as if he is engaged to any of you."

One of the other girls whispered something, and the group turned to stare at Jennet.

She ignored their wide-eyed gawking as she selected her thread packet, and brought it up to the front counter. "I will have this, and some long-eyed needles, please."

The shop keeper smiled uneasily. "Yes, Miss Reed."

"Jennet Reed, is that you?" Rose Abernathy came to join her at the counter. "I thought so. Were you eavesdropping on us? I do not blame you if you were. It is not as if a spinster has anything better to do."

As her friends gasped, she regarded the

smirking girl, but said nothing.

"I will dance with him, you know," Rose assured her, leaning closer. "He is not yours any longer. He has not been for these seven years."

"His lordship is an excellent dancer, so I hope you do," Jennet said, and handed the coins for her purchase to the proprietor. "I would advise you not try to marry him, however. He cannot seem to find the church." To the shopkeeper she said, "Thank you, sir."

Walking out of the shop, Jennet heard Rose sputtering and her friends giggling. It had not been her best retort, she admitted to herself, but she had felt out of sorts ever since learning William Gerard had returned to Renwick. Until he left, there would probably be more of the same, as it seemed no one had forgotten her disastrous engagement.

Of course, they have not. That will be who you are to them for the rest of your days. The spinster, the pariah, the poor girl that William Gerard left at the altar.

The next shop she visited was the dry goods, where she paid for an order Mrs.

Holloway had made, and then decided to treat herself with a stop at the bakery. There she selected some queen cakes, of which she was particularly fond, and a slice of lemon cake with raspberries that her mother loved.

"Miss Reed?" a hesitant voice said.

Jennet turned and saw one of Rose Abernathy's friends hovering behind her. "Excuse me."

When she tried to go around her the girl stepped in her path. "Forgive me," she said quickly. "I know we have not been introduced, but I only wished to apologize."

Jennet nodded and waited.

"My name is Charlotte Fletcher." She bobbed quickly. "We should not have laughed when Rose spoke so rudely to you. I did not know that you had once been engaged to the baron." She ducked her head. "It was very wrong of me."

Despite her contriteness, she seemed on the verge of laughing again.

"Rose sent you to discover if I was crying, I take it?" Jennet asked. As the girl gave her an astonished look, she added, "She also wished you to learn if I had renewed my acquaintance with Baron Greystone, I imagine. I will make your task simple: do assure her I was not, I have not, and I will not."

Charlotte followed her out of the bakery. "How could you know those things?"

Jennet turned on her. "Do you imagine this is the first time I have been ridiculed for what that gentleman did to me? Or no one else has found amusement at my expense? Try, for a moment, to imagine it happened to you. How would you wish to be treated? As cruelly as I have been just now?"

Charlotte looked genuinely ashamed now. "We are not malicious, Miss Reed."

"No, for that would require some effort on your part," she told her. "You are indifferent to the feelings of others. Just as Baron Greystone is. Perhaps *you* should dance with him."

Jennet left her standing and gaping at her, and took her parcels to the rig, stowing them before she climbed up to drive home. She could feel the heat of her anger flushing her face, and willed herself to calm. It served no purpose to become agitated over the things she could never change, like her reputation.

That night after dinner she made up a tray to take the lemon cake to Margaret's room, where she found her mother standing by the window and frowning at something outside.

"Mama, you should be in bed," she reproved lightly as she set down the tray. "What are you looking at?"

"I heard voices," her mother said, and pointed down. "I came over and saw men walking across the property, as bold as you please. The gardeners have already gone home for the day."

"I will tell Barton, and ask him to check the grounds." Jennet helped her mother back to bed before she placed the tray beside her. "Perhaps they were travelers."

"The Romany have gone south, where it is warmer," Margaret told her, and then saw the cake. "What is this? Lemon cake?" She scowled. "Cook did not make this, for we have no lemons, and we ate the last of the berries yesterday. You went to the village."

"I did." Jennet sat down on the edge of

the bed. "I needed some thread, and Mrs. Holloway's order came in. I thought you would enjoy a little treat."

"You cannot distract me with cake," Margaret told her before popping a raspberry into her mouth. "You should have stayed at home, with me. We are about to be cursed."

"I have arranged to avoid any curses." Jennet brushed some of her curls back from her face. "Catherine and I are going to the masquerade at Dredthorne Hall together. She promises not to leave my side for a moment."

Her mother sighed. "That is why you brought the cake, to ease the blow."

"Mama, you leave me little choice. If I go, we will not be cursed," she pointed out. "Catherine will see to it that no one harms me, and I return home safely."

Margaret's bottom lip trembled as she met her gaze. "You think I am a foolish old woman, but I know these things are true. There has been shadow on this family ever since your father died. You should be married now, and a mother, and happy, and you are not."

Jennet took hold of her hands. "I will go to the ball, and try very hard to meet a fine young gentleman. Perhaps he will offer for me, and give me children, and that will make you happy."

"You have never been the same, you know," her mother said softly. "Ever since he left, you have kept your heart locked up against any other. I daresay Wellington himself could offer for you, and you would refuse him."

"His Grace is already married, and rather busy at the moment." She leaned close to whisper, "I have heard that he possesses a hooked nose."

She was finally able to make Margaret laugh, and stayed with her until she finished her cake and was growing drowsy. After she kissed her goodnight, she carried the tray downstairs and mentioned to Mrs. Holloway what Margaret had said about the men wandering on the property.

"They may be poachers, or hands that have lost their positions," the housekeeper said. "I'll ask Barton to have a look tonight, and check the stables and wood shed."

On a hill overlooking the Dredthorne Hall estate, Ruban waited alone beneath an old horse-chestnut tree. The overgrowth that had concealed much of the old house had been cut back, and the rear grounds prepared for a spring garden. In England everything was about appearances, and someone had gone to a great deal of trouble to make the decrepit hall look almost inviting.

While the English danced to music here, others dear to Ruban languished in prisons, or starved in their camps.

A crackle of heavy footsteps through the leaves drew his attention to the large, broad figure approaching him. He wore the heavy, practical garb of a woodsman, but the axe he carried on his shoulder was merely for show. The villagers paid no attention to any common laborers they might see.

Jean-Pierre stopped as soon as he saw the gleam of the pistol and held up his empty hands. "Bonsoir."

"Speak only in English." How many times would he and the other men have to be told that? Ruban felt impatient. "Where are the others?"

"Deep in de woods." The big man jerked his chin in the direction of Dredthorne's back property. "Too cold to sleep on de ground, and we had to leave de other place. Old lady see us. We find a sheep-man's hut."

"Shepherd's hut," Ruban corrected. His English was appalling; perhaps it was better they speak in French.

Jean-Pierre shrugged. "Dat is where we wait for you."

"I will be otherwise engaged." Dropping the heavy haversack at his feet, Ruban nudged it with a boot toe. "Food, enough for three days. Do not light any fires, and stay out of sight until I signal you. Then meet me at the rendezvous point."

He grunted. "You think de Raven will be at de old chateau."

"Oh, yes." Ruban looked at Dredthorne Hall. "Death so enjoys a good party."

CHAPTER 5

Twilight had descended around the weathered grey slate tile roofs and worn buff stone and brick walls of Dredthorne Hall when Baron Greystone stepped out onto the second-floor balcony. A biting wind yanked at his cravat, and raked loose his black mane, determined to dishevel him. Over the years since he had departed Renwick, he had often recalled this old folly, built a century past by a merchant with too much wealth and too little restraint. The previous tenants had made some repairs, mostly to shore up the deteriorating structure and disguise the worst ravages of time, but Pickering had declared it perfectly suited to his scheme.

As he did for all things French,

Greystone felt little admiration for the crumbling would-be chateau, but he would only have to tolerate it for one night. In a handful of hours this thing would be finished, and Greystone could return to London on the morrow.

Not that he especially wished to.

It surprised him how little Renwick had changed since he had left it; the countryside had remained rustic, peaceful and unreservedly charming, just as it had been in his boyhood, in fact. Prior to his arrival he had been obliged to arrange the hiring of more staff for Gerard Lodge in order to make a convincing show of taking up proper residence, but he had already decided to keep them on. His boyhood home had been neglected since his father's illness, and needed to be thoroughly cleaned and refurnished. Once spring came his mother might be persuaded to move to the country, as long as someone else suggested it.

Lady Greystone would have nothing to do with her only son.

I understand you perfectly, William, the baroness had assured him the last time she had spoken to him. *Your father and I raised you to be an honorable gentleman, but you have chosen another path. You also broke the heart of a dear young lady in the worst possible fashion. I only hope your conviction gives you comfort, for you will not have it from us.*

Indeed. He had looked at his father. *You are of the same opinion, sir?*

Nothing more can be said, the baron said, his expression as cold as ever before he turned and left the room.

Before she followed, his mother had taken one long, last look at him. *Please leave this house now, Mr. Gerard, and never again think of returning.*

At his father's funeral six years later, Greystone had watched his mother from the opposite side of the casket. He could see the tracks that tears had left in the rice powder on her cheeks, and the crumpled wad she had made of the handkerchief in her hand. For all his father's coldness his mother had been a devoted, loving wife— just as William had been the silent, obedient son. Not once had the old baron ever attempted to free either of them from the prison of his own making.

Throughout the service Greystone refused to look at the casket holding his father's remains. If he had, he knew he would have kicked it.

When he had tried to approach his mother after the funeral, her maid had stepped in his way, and shaken her head. He had watched as Lady Greystone made her way to a waiting carriage without looking back. The baroness could not even bring herself to acknowledge his presence.

Later, when his father's attorney had met with him alone to discuss his inheritance and the barony, Greystone had given him a letter for his mother. In it he had broken the vow he had made to his father and told her the truth. A day later a footman returned it unopened to him at his club, along with her card, on the back of which she had written three words: Remember your choice.

Besides Greystone, only his father could truly appreciate the irony, but the old baron had gone to his grave as silent on that subject as he had been in life. He'd tossed the letter on the fire and burned his last hope of redemption.

The past wanted to haunt him tonight, Greystone thought as he went to the balcony's railing. Soon the guests for the masquerade ball would arrive, providing what he had been assured would be a distraction essential to the success of their plan. Only after agreeing did he learn that among the guests would be the only woman he had sworn to avoid for the rest of his life.

"We must keep up appearances, and nothing says ordinary like a country dance," Arthur Pickering told him over an after-dinner brandy they had shared during Greystone's first visit to Dredthorne Hall. "I have invited all of the unattached young swains and ladies in Renwick, so there should be a large crowd. Jennet Reed will be among them. Once I have left for London, you may follow on the morrow, unless you have some particular reason to linger."

"None." He kept his expression as bland as Pickering's tone.

"I am gratified to know it will not disturb you to see your jilted bride again," Pickering said. "You will be in costume, so you need not reveal yourself to her. I expect we will all have a marvelous time."

The other man's notion of marvelous encompassed many things Greystone personally despised. "What are you playing at, Arthur?"

"Nothing at all. I enjoy the lady's company, and there's little else in this damned place to provide me with amusement. Not even a decent brothel within riding distance." He toasted him with his snifter. "Never tell me you would have come here without seizing the chance to see her again."

"I never expected nor desired to," Greystone countered. "What would be the point?"

"Precisely." Pickering drained his glass and set it aside. "But my ball will permit you the opportunity to see her without being seen. I am certain that will gratify you in the end. You must be curious. We know you have been making regular inquiries."

The *we* meant London, which boded nothing favorable for Greystone.

A yawn would have been too deliberate

a show of indifference, so he smiled lazily. "You must also be aware that I have inquired after the welfare of my mother, my cousin Germaine and her boys, and some old friends from school." He shook his head. "Have you invited them to your masquerade as well?"

Pickering's eyes narrowed for a moment, and then his expression cleared. "It seems I have overstepped. I am not questioning your steadfastness, old chap. Of all the men I know, you are the most unwavering."

"There was another," Greystone reminded him. "He sacrificed his family on the altar of his loyalty. That is why I will never have one."

"Yet you still make inquiries." Pickering propped his elbows on his knees to lean forward. "Do not glower at me. Until you relinquish the past, you will never be free of the resentment. Had I not been orphaned, I daresay I would have arranged to have my parents believe me dead." He gave him an unpleasant smirk. "Perhaps you should consider the same. Even the most discreet of inquiries can lead to revelations far more unpleasant than the abandonment of a bride."

He shrugged. "My mother would not care if I were dead, and Miss Reed is nothing to me."

Now Greystone stood on the balcony watching for her carriage, that he might see the woman he had dismissed with such callousness. The sight of her would return to him the cold reason he needed for the work, for time would have bestowed much change. He needed to see her dulled and aged by the years, her bloom gone, her innocence giving way to artifice. Perhaps she would resemble her mother now, or have grown stout from consoling herself with sweets. She would be bitter still, and carrying that grudge for so long that it would have etched unkind lines in her face.

Please, God, let her be made plain and dull and forever safe from me.

Footmen came out of the hall to place hollowed turnips on the tops of railings and the sides of steps. Once they had been arranged, tapers were employed to light the candle stubs inside them. The flickering light caused the faces carved through the sides of the turnips to appear appropriately demonic. Snatches of music came faintly from the back of the old chateau as the musicians tuned their instruments in preparation for the dancing. Downstairs the servants would be rushing about to check that all was in readiness; the air would be rosy with the scents of spiced cider and mulled wine. The incomplete renovations to the elderly house gave it the distinct air of being suitably dilapidated and possibly haunted.

Around him the deep violet skies slowly darkened to a charcoal velvet, sheened silver by the rising moon. Greystone heard the first clatter of horses' hooves and creaking of carriage wheels approaching, and drew back into the shadows. The mask Pickering had chosen for him would wholly conceal his features, or so he had assured him. Looking down he counted six carriages, each stopping in turn to reveal their occupants.

In the city, elegant dress and artful masks would have been expected, but here in the country the guests dressed in true costumes. He saw the men of Renwick wearing old uniforms, outdated livery, and even some monks' robes. Their ladies had garbed themselves in fashions of decades past, and sparkled with paste-gemmed tiaras, necklaces and ear bobs. Their smiling faces and shared laughter made him feel a thousand years older.

Like his mother, they would never know about his dark inheritance, or how often he had washed the blood of it from his hands.

Two young women then climbed down from a rig in vintage ball gowns so voluminous they seemed to float like clouds. Ghosts of fashions long past, they shimmered in the scant light. Each wore a velvet mask that covered enough of the face to conceal their identities, and lent them the air of refined criminals. The taller of the two moved into a pool of glowing amber from the turnips' candles, which gilded her blue gown and awoke the dark fire of her auburn hair. That color had been burned into Greystone's memory as a winter bonfire that could never be extinguished.

There, she has come.

Greystone watched Jennet Reed lift her skirts to mount the steps leading up to the hall. She still moved with the same easy poise, her head held high, her movements effortless. Although the full gown tried to disguise her body, he could tell that her long-limbed form remained as slender as it ever had been. He had no doubt she would still smell of rose water and almond oil from the cream she used to keep her hands smooth. Touching her skin had been the same as caressing sun-warmed silk. It still would be, he imagined.

Jennet appeared no older than any debutante in her first season, and yet he knew her to be close to thirty now. How could she look so unchanged?

We will grow old together, she had said to Greystone just after she had accepted his proposal of marriage. *How do you think you will like me when I am bent over and wrinkled and smell of rheumatism balm?*

He had laughed at her. *Who do you expect will be rubbing you down with that balm, my heart?*

Below him Jennet's brows arched as she paused and regarded the faces of the carved turnips. From the thinning of her lips she didn't care for the devilish decorations.

Greystone tensed, and then wondered why he did. If she left in a huff Pickering would be disappointed, but he would be spared the torment of watching her from afar. If she stayed he would spend the rest of the night yearning to hear her voice, look into her eyes, and kiss her until her knees gave way.

Her effect on him had not changed, it seemed. Despite his claims to Pickering, and his own futile wishes, he would always be obsessed with her. Greystone imagined that as fitting punishment. He deserved much worse.

The other young lady then said something to her, and Jennet's expression shifted from dislike to wry amusement. As another quartet of costumed guests joined them, the pair fell into a lively conversation. She seemed content to be part of the group, and listen as the others chattered away, just as she always had in the past.

Nothing had changed her.

Seven years ago, Greystone had done to Jennet the very worst thing possible. He had driven out of Renwick, past the church where at that very moment she waited to marry him, and took the road to London. When he stopped to water and rest his horses, he had almost turned around to go back. Saner thoughts prevailed, and he continued on to his parents' house in Mayfair. Once he had finished making the necessary arrangements to travel, he had gone to his club. There he had gotten so drunk he'd spent most of the night casting up his accounts.

A few days later he had left England, not to return for three years.

The weight of knowing what he had done to Jennet had been the only burden from his old life that Greystone had never been able to shed. By jilting her so abruptly he knew he had snuffed out any tender feeling she'd had for him; that had been his intent. No, he had wanted her to hate him with all her heart. He would have spared her the public humiliation of being left at the altar, but that, too, had been imperative. After his ruination of her Jennet had never married, that much he had allowed himself to glean from various sources familiar with the Reeds.

He had not simply ruined her; he had

condemned her to a life of solitude and misery. Any man tempted by Jennet would be swiftly told of Greystone's abandonment. No matter how much a man was to blame for a broken engagement, society held the rejected lady responsible. Aside from estranging himself from his parents, condemning a bright, beautiful young woman to the narrow, joyless existence of a spinster had been what Greystone considered his most singularly despicable act.

Yet here she was, Miss Jennet Reed, stepped out of his past into his present, seemingly without a single alteration. Smiling and easy with her friends, as if she had never suffered a moment in her life. Obviously prepared to dance and enjoy herself, was Jennet. She behaved as if she had not a care in the world. Greystone looked down and saw he had gripped the balcony railing so tightly his knuckles had gone white.

Was he angry with her for carrying on without him so brilliantly? It seemed so.

"Excuse me, my lord," a nervous voice

said from behind him. "You're wanted downstairs."

Greystone turned to see one of Pickering's aides hovering just inside the chamber, a small bundle in his hands. He walked inside and took the mask, glowering as he held it up for inspection. It would conceal his face, just as his friend had promised. It would also make him look the fool, but perhaps that was exactly what he was.

Jennet Reed had survived him, and now he had other matters to attend to.

"Tell Pickering I'll join him in a moment," Greystone said to the servant as he gathered up his hair to tie it in a queue.

Once the man had left he stepped into the dressing room, moving aside the wash stand before kneeling. From the satchel he had hidden under the floor boards he took the only item of true significance he had brought with him to Renwick. It looked so ordinary; no one would give it a second glance. Pickering would call it the embodiment of hope, but it should have been dripping with the blood of all the men who had died so that Greystone might possess it.

What would happen if he took it into the bed chamber and tossed it into the fireplace? To do so would seal his own fate just as surely—but for a moment he longed for that finality. To be done with it all. To surrender himself to the darkness completely.

Remember your choice.

Greystone slipped his last hope into his boot, right next to the blade he used to cut throats.

CHAPTER 6

The moment the carriage drew within sight of Dredthorne Hall's aged walls and lamplit windows Jennet felt the oddest sense of being watched by the mansion. Naturally she had seen the old house before tonight, but only in glimpses from her rig while out driving. As with all places of dark reputation Dredthorne seemed menacing, especially in how it loomed ever larger, blotting out the stars and moon. By the time their driver reined in the horses to stop before the wide steps of the front entry Jennet felt reduced to the size of a mouse gazing up at a mammoth.

I see you, Dredthorne Hall seemed to whisper. *Come inside...if you dare.*

"You are being ridiculous," Jennet muttered under her breath.

Catherine turned to frown at her. "What was that?"

"The house," she said, feeling silly now. "It appears quite, ah, ominous."

"Of course, it does." Her friend adjusted her mask. "Mr. Pickering likely rented the place precisely to set the correct tone for the ball. Atmosphere is everything these days, my dear. You should see what the Regent has done to the Pavilion at Brighton."

Arthur Pickering likely thought it amusing to hold the masquerade in a house believed to be haunted by the souls of those who had died within its walls, Jennet thought. Although all of the deaths had been accidental, the gossips in the village had whispered of murders made to appear thus. She could see he had arranged carved turnip lanterns on every step, like so many little decapitated heads. Looking into their fiery eyes made her stomach clench as tightly as her gloved hands. Perhaps others would think it great fun, but to her it now seemed a ghastly notion.

"Are you not feeling well?" Jennet heard Catherine ask once they had alighted from the carriage. "You look pale."

"I am a little chilled." She dragged her attention from the wee grimacing turnips to regard her friend. While they had been talking with the Carstairs sisters and their escorts, a line of newly-arrived guests had formed on the steps. Politeness obliged them to move to the end of it, but they would soon be inside at the receiving line. "I should have worn my cloak."

"I see I must inspect your wardrobe, and relieve you of anything that might tempt you to commit such a *faux pas*," her friend chided as she stood on her toes to look over the heads of the guests in front of them. "I believe Mr. Pickering is greeting everyone. Look, he's dressed himself as a straw man and put a sack over his head. Such an improvement."

"Be kind," Jennet chided. "This is not London, you know."

As a black cat leapt from the shrubbery to dart between them and across the drive, Catherine drew back her skirts. "It certainly is not."

Her friend's disdain helped disperse most of her trepidation, but Jennet still kept a wary eye on the house. Two more couples called out greetings as they joined them, and she forced herself to smile and laugh as if they were meeting at the village hall for a country dance.

"My grandmother insists that this house is cursed," one of the gentlemen told them in a hushed tone. "Every master of Dredthorne Hall is doomed to fall in love with a lady who spends the night. Once they are married, his wife in turn will either go mad or die within the first year."

"What nonsense." Catherine sniffed. "That could not possibly happen, unless Dredthorne's masters have all been exceptionally gullible bachelors, and exceedingly boring husbands, of course."

Jennet laughed along with everyone, but the remark brought back how she had been, immediately after being left at the altar. Anyone who had seen what she had done to her wedding gown would have regarded her as not entirely sane. Thankfully that brush with madness had been of very short duration, and never again returned. She had not been cursed by her duplicitous lover; she had been set free of him.

"Ladies, I have a notion to elude this curse," Catherine was saying, "All we need do is avoid becoming engaged to Mr. Pickering, and leave well before the midnight hour." She smiled at Jennet. "My dear friend here has become expert at both, so we must hope she demonstrates her talents."

"Oh, the trick is quite simple," Jennet told them. "Simply say no, and go."

Once safely inside Dredthorne Hall Jennet eyed the receiving line. Of the four costumed hosts welcoming the arrivals, just one stood tall enough to be Arthur Pickering. Only he would be so ridiculous as to wear a sacking mask, and rough old clothes liberally adorned with bits of hay, in order to emulate a straw man. Yet the longer Jennet regarded him the more startled she felt. Why had she never before noticed how broad his shoulders were, or those bulges of muscle along his arms? Either he had stuffed more hay under his costume, or his tailor had been doing him a terrible disservice.

She bided her time, smiling and nodding to the other hosts before halting in front of the straw man and poking her fan in his ribs the moment he straightened from his bow.

"I do not appreciate your invitation, sir," Jennet told him firmly. "The wording you employed quite scared my mother out of her wits. I insist you issue any future messages to me without the threat of curses on my family, or I will replace my fan with a club."

The straw man took hold of her wrist, and drew her hand up to his mask to press it against the crookedly-sewn seam serving as his mouth.

Feeling the warmth and pressure of his lips through the sacking sent a jolt of sensation through Jennet. The heated wave sizzled along her skin before sinking deep into her breast. For a moment everyone around her faded into ghosts of themselves as she stared at Pickering's bent, masked head and saw instead gleaming black hair tied neatly in a queue.

That kiss had been bestowed on what Jennet had considered the most exciting night of her life, and what she regarded now as the greatest mistake she had ever made.

AT THE TIME attending the annual village harvest dance hadn't tempted Jennet, who preferred to stay home with her mother after the summer waned and the days grew shorter. She knew Margaret hated the cold, and without some distraction would grow melancholic. Together they spent the evenings sewing, playing cards or reading together. Often her mother would badger her on getting out to socialize, however, and on that occasion she had insisted.

"You have been shut in this house with me too long, my dear," Margaret said. "I daresay Catherine Tindall and your other friends will be there. All of the young men in Renwick will wish to dance with you, I am sure."

Jennet frowned at her. "Why are you so set on this, Mama? I have never been fond of going out in society."

"But that is where you can be with

people your own age," her mother said, sounding slightly exasperated now. "You need not worry about me. I mean to change the ribbons on my good church bonnet, and I have the new Edgeworth novel to read. I do hope it is as scandalous as Lady Hardiwick claimed. Now, please, go, and enjoy yourself."

Held at the spacious hall in the heart of Renwick, the harvest dance attracted most of the younger set. Jennet hovered outside for a moment to peer in through the windows and see if Catherine and her friends had arrived. That was when she overheard the conversation among a group of bachelors who had congregated just on the other side.

"I vow I saw her driving herself here," one of the young men said. "She is wearing dark velvet, and comes alone. I hardly ever see her out in society. I must ask her to dance as soon as she makes an appearance."

"Do you mean Jennet Reed?" another man asked, his upper lip curling. "As dour as a dowager, that one, and twice as prim."

Jennet recognized her disparager. He had made a nuisance of himself at another assembly, simply because she had refused to dance with him.

"She refused to dance with you, I take it?" a tall, dark-haired gentleman inquired, as if he had heard her thoughts. When the other man scowled, he said, "A shame, then, that the lady has good taste."

She moved to the other side of the window to get a better look at her defender's face, and saw it was William Gerard. She had been introduced to him years ago, while he had been on holiday from school. At the time she had been a skinny girl of ten with dark red braids and very little to say, mostly out of embarrassment. In those days Margaret had dressed her like a doll, usually in fussy lace gowns that made her resemble a moth cocoon with legs.

I like your eyes much more than my own, Jennet remembered William saying to her. *Shall we trade?*

William had changed greatly since that brief meeting. The lanky, polite older boy she remembered had grown tall and broad-shouldered, and dressed in the latest fashions for men without looking foppish.

He greatly resembled his father in coloring and features, but did not share the baron's perpetually stern expression. His dark green eyes seemed to smile even when his mouth didn't.

Jennet felt mesmerized.

Of course, every unattached young lady inside the hall was discreetly watching the dark, handsome heir to the Greystone barony; William's father was enormously wealthy as well as a peer of the realm. His son would someday inherit all of it, including a grand house in London as well as Gerard Lodge, a magnificent Georgian mansion on an expansive estate, making him quite the eligible bachelor. From the polished perfection of his appearance he also possessed, as her friend Catherine would say, town bronze.

She would go home this moment, Jennet decided, turning away. The last thing she needed was to spend the night mooning over a man she had met exactly once. Yet before she could take a step the door to the hall opened, making her step back.

William Gerard came outside, closing the door and blocking her path. Jennet pivoted, intending to go the other way, when his voice stopped her.

"Miss Reed." As she turned, he bowed to her. "I have not seen you at church all month. Are you become a heathen?"

Jennet bobbed. When she lifted her chin to meet his gaze she started to reply, and then a shaft of light from the setting sun fell over them, gilding William with the softest, purest glow. He looked so resplendent in that moment she forgot her manners, her sensibility, everything.

"Where have you been?" she murmured, although her own words made absolutely no sense to her.

He looked all over her face. "Trying to find you." He sounded as dazed as she felt.

The music and voices from within the hall dwindled away as William matched her silence and stillness with his own. Looking at him made Jennet wonder why she had ever bothered to do anything else. She imagined standing in that spot and gazing at him for years; she would not consider the time wasted. It could not happen this way, she thought in some distant corner of her mind, and yet it was. It had.

"You look so much like your father," Jennet finally said, shocked again by how her voice sounded now, as if it came from her heart rather than her throat. "And yet, you are nothing at all like him."

"You could not have offered a more perfect complement," he said, smiling a little. "I miss your braids, but not the lace. Will you come and dance with me, Miss Reed?"

"I am not inclined to, Mr. Gerard, and with you…" She swallowed and cleared her throat. "Perhaps it would not be wise."

"I would agree, but I cannot help myself. You bewitch me." William took hold of her hand, bowing down to press his mouth against her knuckles. "Shall we be foolish, then?"

* * *

THE MEMORY of meeting William Gerard for the first time faded as the straw man straightened, and Jennet came back to her senses.

"You are an unrepentant cad, Mr.

Pickering." She turned and marched after Catherine into the reception room.

As the assembled guests milled around them, Jennet took in her surroundings. The oval room's curving walls had been repainted a snowy white, but she could see hints of older, slightly foxed paint in the nooks and curls of the ornate molding. The hundreds of crystals on both of the grand chandeliers had been cleaned, but a few dusty cobwebs still decorated the upper tiers between the sparkling prisms, likely left for the haunting effect. Long tables draped in damask and linen held punch bowls filled with spiced cider, and pitchers brimming with mulled wine encircled by rows of polished silver goblets.

"You look splendid, my dears," an older woman told Jennet and Catherine, and then leaned closer to say in a much lower voice, "If you mean to imbibe, you should know our host has prepared a retiring room on the second floor." She hurried off to speak to another group of new arrivals.

"Ah, the rustic nature of country manners." Catherine gave her a rueful look. "In London no one at a ball tells you where you may find a chamber pot. I suppose that is why we ladies refrain from imbibing."

Jennet smiled. "Now that you know, you may drink as much as you like, but I would advise you keep to the cider."

"If you find me in my cups, then you may send me home." Her friend looked over at a group of young men and giggled. "But not too soon, please."

They took a turn around the reception room so that Catherine could attempt to guess which of the guests they knew. Jennet silently corrected her speculations as she used her talent for observation to determine their identities. The vicar and his wife, both short of stature and staying well away from the wine, had dressed appropriately as a shepherd and shepherdess. The Brexley spinsters Jennet recognized from their costumes as Selene, goddess of the moon, and Eos, goddess of the dawn, also sisters. They had also retreated to a corner where they might watch and whisper to each other, which is what they did at every party they attended.

"I cannot believe that Rose Abernathy thought to dress as Marie Antionette,"

Catherine complained as they finished their circuit, and glared back at the lady in question. "It is positively traitorous—and to wear a robe de gaulle to a ball, of all things. That dress is little more than an over-long chemise."

Jennet surveyed Miss Abernathy, whose airy white cotton gown looked quite comfortable compared to the stiff silk of her own costume. She had also foregone the expected powdered wig in favor of a wide-brimmed straw hat decorated with a few silvery plumes. Yet she knew what lay beneath all that finery, thanks to the unpleasant encounter she'd had with her at the haberdasher's shop.

"I believe she imitates a rather famous portrait of the queen," Jennet told her friend. "I imagine young ladies who have not lost a relative to war still admire her sense of style."

"I have reminded you of your poor father, how wretched of me." Catherine gave her a rueful look. "I should not revile her. Someday this war will end, Jennet, and our men will come home victorious at last."

"Until the next war breaks out." Jennet

felt an odd sensation of being watched, and resisted the urge to inspect everyone near them. "Do you see Mr. Pickering?"

"Not since we came through the line." Her friend stood on her toes and looked around them before she pointed at the front of the reception room. "There, he is just leaving."

"I will return in a moment," she told Catherine before heading after him.

She caught a glimpse of the straw man as she came out into the center hall, but as she turned to the right all she saw was a wall painted with a large, faded chinoiserie depiction of a garden beyond a white iron fence. As she turned away she saw a shadow appear on the painting, and went closer to discover a pair of door handles painted in such a way to look like part of the gate.

"Very clever," Jennet murmured as she tugged on one handle, opening a door-size panel in the painting that led into another room. She stepped inside.

The scent of beeswax came from an elaborate silver candelabra in the center of the long dining table. It held a handful of candles that partially illuminated the remarkable décor of the room. Every wall had been fitted with a carved, inlaid panel of dark wood painted with murals. Between them very fine marble columns rose to the ceiling, giving an effect of standing inside a temple.

Jennet picked up the candelabra and carried it over to the nearest panel, which had been painted with a mostly-nude, very strong-looking ancient warrior holding three golden apples in his hand. Behind him three ladies resembling rather peevish nymphs glared at the back of his head. It reminded her so much of the scene with Rose Abernathy she smiled.

"I know precisely how you feel," she murmured. "I had what they coveted, didn't I?" Or at least she had for a time.

The door behind her creaked as the shepherd cautiously entered.

"Forgive me the intrusion," he said, bowing to her. "I thought I might slip in unnoticed to admire the panels." He glanced around, his mouth bowing. "Why, this is incredible."

"I think it a tribute to the labors of Herakles, Vicar," she told him. "He was set the task of stealing the sacred apples from the Hesperides. It required quite an effort on his part, as I recall."

"Yes, in pursuit of his prize Atlas tricked him into holding up the world for him, at least until he duped the god into removing it from his shoulders." Jeffrey Branwen removed his mask. "I am glad you recognized me, Miss Reed. I had hoped to speak to you again in less crowded company."

"So, I have not deceived you, either," she said as she tugged down her mask.

He chuckled. "Your costume is very good, but you did not conceal your hair. No one else in my parish possesses such a singular shade of red."

Jennet already knew why he wished to talk to her. "Miss Tindall told me that William Gerard has returned to Renwick, or I should say, Baron Greystone. I believe he is to attend the masquerade tonight as well. That is why you followed me into this room, is it not?"

The vicar nodded. "I have no desire to pry, my dear girl, only to offer my consolation, if you have need of it. Or a willing ear. Often it is good to talk to someone when such unhappy situations arise."

"Have you known me to be in such need of late?" Jennet asked.

"No," Jeffrey admitted. "I am not satisfied that I did enough for you after William left. There has always lingered an uneasiness in me on that account."

A week after Jennet had been abandoned by her betrothed, the vicar had called at Reed Park. A sensitive man, he had probably thought to give her time to get over the first, worst part of being jilted. She remembered sitting with him and Margaret, cradling a cup of tea until it went stone cold, and hardly saying a word to either of them. That tableau had been repeated several times.

"You were very attentive, and a great help to my mother," she told him. "I am sorry I was so silent at the time. I fear I had nothing to say that would have been acceptable or even rational. Indeed, I spent the first week imagining how I might kill him if he ever returned."

He nodded, completely unperturbed by

her malevolent admission. "Knife in the back, or a bullet through the heart?"

"Poisoning," Jennet said. "Much tidier, and I would not have to be there."

"I have been pushed to such thoughts myself on one or two occasions." Jeffrey glanced at Herakles before he said, "Often life demands of us heroic effort in the worst of circumstances. I think that is when we are most capable of it, and when we become the best versions of ourselves. That I learned from my dear sister, Lucetta, who is quite a hundred times the best of heroes."

"You are fortunate." She thought of the ugly scene she'd had with Charlotte Fletcher. "It is not always possible to be a hero and human. Sometimes we become the worst instead of the best."

"Happily, there is almost always another chance to prove ourselves otherwise." He offered her his arm. "May I escort you back to the ball?"

CHAPTER 7

When Jennet returned with the vicar to the reception room, she noticed an older woman wrapped in a colorful shawl sat on one side of a small, black-draped table by the hearth. An embroidered scarf tied back her frizzed hair from the face she had painted so heavily it looked like a crackled mask. A pair of wide-eyed young ladies, whom Jennet recognized as two of her neighbors' youngest daughters, sat on the other side of the table. Between them and the older woman lay a battered deck of tarot cards.

"Alas, despite my best efforts there remains much enthusiasm for certain pagan practices," Jeffrey said to her. "And my dear wife now looks ready to dance, or smack me with her crook. I should attend to the former before she resorts to the latter. Enjoy your evening, Miss Reed." He bowed and then headed across the room.

Jennet remained where she stood to watch the fortune-teller. During the summers a band of Romany were permitted to encamp at Reed Park when hired to help with the sheep shearing, thanks to Jennet's mother, who had a soft spot for the nomadic people. Every year Margaret would take her to the field where they kept their gaily-painted caravan wagons. There she would greet their ladies and assure they had all they needed for their families. From that long familiarity Jennet knew the travelers to be mannerly and quiet. They dressed in practical garments and kept to themselves.

If this florid fortune-teller had been born a Romany, Jennet would dine on her velvet domino.

Beyond the reception room lively dancing music played. Jennet looked for Catherine, only to see her friend engaged by a handsome young man a short distance away. Before she could catch her eye Catherine took the man's arm and walked with him in the direction of the music. She should follow them, she thought, but glanced again at the fortune-teller, who now had both of the young debutantes hanging on her every word.

Unlike the Romany, who were the cleanest people Jennet had ever encountered, this traveler had a line of grime under her chin, and black-rimmed fingernails.

Jennet seethed silently as she watched the reading progress. The woman's exaggerated gestures and frequent leanings over the table seemed more suited to the stage than the telling of fortunes. The manner in which she dealt out the cards seemed highly suspect as well. When the fortune-teller took one of the girls' hands in hers and leaned closer to whisper to her, Jennet recognized her game.

Oh, this would not do.

She watched until the fortune-teller finished the reading, and the giggling girls left the table. Only then did she approach. "Good evening, Madam."

"Milady. I am Masilda," she said in a stilted accent, and gestured toward one of the chairs. "Please, join me, and I will read the cards for you, for free."

"I should pay you something for your trouble." Jennet reached down as if to hand her a coin, and then reached into the fortune-teller's wide sleeve. As the would-be Romany stiffened, she pulled out the bracelet she had seen her slip from the girl's wrist. "Or perhaps not. You appear to be doing quite well for yourself."

Masilda recoiled, and scowled. "That I have never seen."

"Fortunately, I have." She nodded in the direction of the two debutantes. "This bracelet belonged to that young lady's grandmother, who left it to her after she passed away last year. She was quite proud to show it to me when last she wore it to church. She would be heartbroken to discover it stolen."

"I stole nothing," Masilda protested. "It must have fallen from her arm."

"As I imagine many such baubles do in your presence." Jennet looked into the thief's eyes, and let her own go steely. "Mr.

Pickering did not hire you to steal from his guests. I suggest you leave at once, or I will summon the footmen to escort you directly to the magistrate."

The fortune-teller grabbed the tarot cards and shoved them into the front of her bodice as she got to her feet.

"You watch, me fine lady," Masilda said in a harsh Cockney accent, her lips curling into a sneer. "Before this dance is done, you will see your own death."

Jennet would have laughed as the fortune-teller scurried out of the reception room, but the thieving charlatan's prediction gave her pause. Unlike the rest of the Reed family, she herself had never been reckless. Indeed, she now devoted herself to living a very quiet life free of heedless impulses. Her demise, eventual as it had to be, had never greatly concerned her. Jennet had imagined dying only at an advanced age, possibly of boredom, definitely alone.

Only she did not wish to die alone, or tonight at the ball. But why would Masilda predict such a ghastly thing? Had she hoped to scare her in retaliation for being exposed as a thief?

"How do you do, Miss Reed?" a man said from behind her.

Turning to behold a tall highwayman ably disguised by a grinning mask, Jennet dropped into a polite curtsey. Too scattered in thought to surmise his identity, she said, "You have guessed my name, sir. Are we acquainted?"

He bowed in return before he pulled up the mask, revealing his long, narrow face and placid brown eyes. "Arthur Pickering, at your service."

She regarded his costume. "Were you not earlier dressed as a straw man, sir?"

"No, that was an old friend. I thought you might have guessed when I greeted you at the door." He glanced at the fortune-teller's table. "I fear there will be no more readings tonight. One of the footmen reported seeing the Romany lady fleeing the house."

"That woman was as much a traveler as I am." She showed him the bracelet as she related what the fortune-teller had done, and her own threat, adding, "I expect it was high-handed of me to order her to leave, but I did not wish to create a scene unpleasant to your guests. I daresay you would have done the same."

"Indeed, and I thank you for your diligence." Pickering's expression grew sly. "You are rumored to be quite the diviner, Miss Reed."

"I am nothing of the sort." Still, she had chased off his would-be fortune-teller, and Jennet felt some obligation for that. "However, if you will bring to me playing cards, I will stand in for your entertainment and provide some readings for your guests."

He beamed as he reached into his cloak, and withdrew a boxed deck. "I have anticipated your generosity."

GREYSTONE TOOK up a stance at one side of the reception hall where he could watch every entrance and exit while keeping his back to the curved wall. The chandeliers shed pooled light, allowing him to stand in a pocket of shadow. That position also gave him the perfect vantage point to watch Jennet Reed as she sat down by the hearth.

She had seemed genuinely surprised to discover Pickering behind the highwayman's idiotic mask, which gratified and annoyed him.

Staring at her as much as he wished made him want a dark, empty room and that long, lovely throat clasped between his hands.

To shut out the sight of her, Greystone closed his eyes, which proved a grave mistake. From the locked and chained trunks of his memory escaped an image of a meadow filled with daisies and dandelions just beyond the gardens surrounding his family's country home. That afternoon had been one of the best of his life.

In the center of the fragrant, colorful profusion of blooms Jennet sat on a blue and green plaid, patiently watching as he finished unpacking the picnic hamper. He had been talking of the improvements he wished to make to the lodge, and a hot house he meant to build. When they married, he had explained, he wished Jennet to have the strawberries she loved whenever she liked. Then he had looked up to see her frown, her face flushed and her green eyes sparkling as if with temper.

You think it too frivolous, Miss Reed?

Strawberries are very nice. Jennet reached for his hand, and boldly twined her fingers through his. *What I want most is you, Mr. Gerard.*

That shameless confession had proved his undoing. He had pulled her into his arms and kissed her, and the taste of her lips had made him even wilder. She had not protested or struggled; she returned his passion with an equal measure of her own, just as she had under the kissing bough at Christmas. If the baroness had not walked down from the lodge to join them a few moments later, Greystone would have surely taken her right there in the flower-speckled grass, under the bright July sun. He remembered how his mother had laughed as they quickly ended the heated embrace.

That can wait until the two of you are wed, my lad.

He forced his attention back to the other guests, all of whom he easily identified despite their masks. He saw childhood friends now grown into adults, many paired off as couples. They seemed to him so blissfully unaware of anything beyond their modest scope. Greystone also realized that life had gone on in Renwick without him, which gave him a curiously empty feeling. None of Pickering's guests would ever know what William Gerard had become, or why, and that was as it should be. Still, for a moment he wished he could truly unmask himself in every sense of the word. It would horrify them to know the truth, but it would change their perception of the woman he had so ruthlessly abandoned.

She would be congratulated instead of pitied.

Prudence Hardiwick arrived with a large group of her giggling friends, all of whom had dressed as various members of royalty. After helping themselves to the wine most of them hurried off to the ballroom, obviously eager to dance. Prudence stayed behind to approach Jennet.

"Are you telling fortunes tonight?" she asked. "If you are you should have a crystal ball, you know. It is just the thing now."

Jennet shuffled the deck effortlessly as she looked up at Prudence. "I find the cards a more reliable source. Would you care for a reading?"

Greystone felt amused as he watched Prudence sit down and his former betrothed select cards at random and lay them out on the table. Jennet had some skill in cartomancy; she had demonstrated it to him and his parents on more than one occasion. Yet the lady's real gift came from her keen observations of others.

"Six of spades," Jennet said to Prudence, tapping the first card she put down between them. "This means that you long for an alteration in your situation."

That provoked a giggle. "Oh, yes, ever since my last season in London."

Jennet nodded and placed another card on the table. "The jack of clubs. You have a young admirer who has taken an interest in your future."

"That would be Peter Mason, poor dear. He is so awfully amusing, and only four years younger than me." Prudence sighed. "I wish we could spend more time together, but since his sister has been widowed … " She shook her head.

"This is the card of jealousy," Jennet said as she put a five of hearts next to the jack. "Someone resents this change in your life."

"Not Mama, certainly," Prudence said, and then her expression shifted into a scowl. "Peter's sister has been unbearably proper since our introduction. She will not permit us to sit together alone whenever I call. She even told him he could not come to the ball with me."

"Two of clubs." Jennet watched the other woman's face. "Your future happiness depends on how you deal with the obstacle that comes between you and your heart's desire."

Prudence frowned. "I cannot remove his sister."

"The card does not represent a person, but a problem." Picking up the cards, Jennet returned them to the deck. "Something you enjoy indulging in now should be made absent from your situation."

The other woman drew back. "Surely not attending balls and assemblies. I should die of dreariness." She thought for a moment. "There is ever so much talk about me."

"Is this talk kind?" Jennet asked, and then when Prudence grimaced she said, "Then you have named your obstacle."

"I must go and speak with Morwena. She is the worst gossip, and always telling tales about me," the Hardiwick girl said, and hurried off.

Greystone almost laughed out loud. While she had displayed the cards, Jennet's interpretations of them came more from the Hardiwick girl's reactions. She still possessed the uncanny ability to judge people by their expressions, which she demonstrated just as admirably with the next four guests who sat down for a reading.

"She is a marvel, your girl," Arthur Pickering murmured as he joined him. "I believe I will ask her to marry me again before we return to London tonight."

"She is not my girl, and you are wed to your work." Greystone considered clouting his companion on the ear, and then realized what he had said. "I am riding with you now?"

"London sent word. They intercepted a message that contains a mention of Renwick and the Raven," Pickering said in a lower voice. "I expect the French have already sent hunters to search for the black bird. Perhaps even that bastard Ruban himself."

The most infamous criminal in England, Ruban had never been seen by any man still breathing. Those who encountered the Frenchman in person had been murdered before they could identify him. Others in pursuit of him had suddenly gone missing without a trace, including one of Greystone's oldest allies, now presumed dead.

"I should very much like to stay," Greystone said through his teeth, "that I might greet him in the flesh."

Pickering made a tsking sound. "There you go, thinking only of yourself and your wonts, you selfish prig. You forget that I am but the messenger. I will need you to watch my back."

"Very well." His gaze went back to the women at the table. "I will do as you say. Only leave Miss Reed alone."

"How intriguing. I recall you saying she is nothing to you." Through his mask Pickering's placid brown eyes turned as sharp and clever as a fox's. "After all this time and distance, the flame of true love yet burns." He laughed.

Greystone saw Jennet turn her head toward the sound to regard them both. "You've made her notice us."

His partner in crime elbowed him neatly. "You did that when she arrived and you nearly devoured her hand, you idiot. Jennet Reed can never be yours. Remember that, and your purpose." He strode toward an older couple. "Lord Kellworth, quite delighted to see you. Might I steal your lovely wife for the next dance?"

Pickering's warning of Jennet Reed, *can never be yours,* blurred into Lady Greystone's soft voice saying *Remember your choice.*

Greystone met Jennet's gaze, which had not wavered from him. He realized that he had somehow stepped out of the shadows without being aware of his own movement, and now he was walking to her. Her brows arched as he approached, but otherwise she remained still and watchful. He took the chair across from her, and gestured toward the cards in her hands.

She took in a quick breath and then scowled. "I have no need to deal the cards for you, sir," she said crisply. "You are as transparent as water to me."

Greystone barely heard her, entranced to be close enough to touch her again. He could smell the sweetness of rose water and almond oil from her skin, and beneath that her own intoxicating scent. The glow from the hearth made her hair look like banked embers coming to life again. Her eyes shone with the cool green of priceless jade and the growing heat of anger. By God, she was all fire and beauty, as alluring as if their years apart had dwindled to as many days.

He could say nothing. If he spoke, she would know him.

Jennet slapped down the deck. "As you have nothing to say, permit me to offer you some advice, sir. Lying jackals always come to bad ends. If one particular cur, whom I will never forgive, chose to pointlessly beleaguer me, I should kill him dead."

Greystone watched her rise and march

out through the garden doors. Pickering was right, he thought as he stood. He truly was an idiot.

CHAPTER 8

Jennet stopped at the glass doors at the back of the reception room, and looked out at the terraced gardens. The fury she felt did not want to subside. Indeed, it still swelled in her breast like some internal fire stoked by the outrageous desire she had seen in the straw man's dark green eyes. The shadowy emerald shade of his gaze had been unmistakable, and brought back an echo of something he had said once to her.

We will have green-eyed children, I expect. May our girls be as bewitching as their mother.

You will change your mind on that, she had told him, *when our daughters come of age.*

Even after all he had done to ruin her life and trample her heart and destroy her innocence, William Gerard had returned to Renwick—and he still wanted her. She knew she should summon a carriage and go home before she did something she would genuinely regret. She did not wish to join the dismal ranks of the legendary mistresses of Dredthorne and go mad.

Oh, but she could beat that horrid, spiteful swine of a man until his skull cracked, and never lose another moment's peace over it.

Yanking open the door, Jennet walked out into the cold night air. It made every breath she took too sharp for comfort, but she welcomed the chill. Hopefully it would erase this blazing flush that had crawled up her neck into her face. Quickly she marched down the steps, determined to put as much distance between her and her tormentor as she could until she calmed.

How could he do this to her? She had been finished with him. Done. He had been forgotten entirely.

You came here hoping to see him, her sensibility whispered. *Admit it.*

Jennet came to the end of the paved pathway sooner than she expected, and stopped to survey her surroundings. Idly she fanned herself as she considered her prospects. She might continue through the fields beyond, for the moon had bathed them in silvery light. The shadowy outlines of a small building to her right suggested it to be a hot house, where she might conceal herself until her temper subsided, and she felt more like herself again. Even now her nape tingled madly, as if he were standing just behind her–

Jennet spun around to see the straw man striding rapidly toward her. She would have to keep up the pretense another moment, it seemed.

"Return to the ball, sir," she told him, closing her fan with a snap. She felt proud of the haughty indifference in her tone. "I have finished with readings for the night."

He came too close, and caught her arm when she would have passed around him. First he pulled away her mask, tossing it aside, and then tugged off the sacking shrouding his head. That confirmed her suspicions irrefutably.

Greystone was the straw man.

Jennet took in the measure of her

former love. He seemed much older than the young man she had known. New lines bracketed his mouth and rayed out from the corners of his eyes; a small scar divided one of his winged brows. Streaks of silver glinted in the black hair at his temples, making him look more like this father than ever. The beard shadow that blued his jawline appeared quite heavier. His mouth had thinned and grown harder; his eyes had become hooded. He had been everything handsome when he had promised to wed her, but now he looked too big and battered to be William Gerard.

What he looked like was dangerous.

"Miss Reed."

"Baron Greystone." Jennet would not curtsey to him even if all of her leg bones snapped, but there was no one to witness her rudeness. "Pray excuse me. My friends will be wondering where I have got to."

"A moment, please." His voice had grown softer and deeper over the years, and brushed like silk velvet against her ears. "I wish to speak to you."

Of course, he did. What he assumed he had was her interest, which she should squash this moment. "We have nothing to say to each other, sir."

"You need only listen." He hesitated before he took his hand from her arm. "I apologize, Miss Reed, for leaving you at the church. Please understand that I never intended to do you harm."

Sorry. He was sorry.

Jennet stared at him. For the life of her she could not imagine why he would say such a thing. The man who had fled Renwick for parts unknown, never to return until tonight, thought he must now express regret to her. The lover who had convinced her to accept his heart before smashing hers so thoroughly, had decided to offer an apology. The cad who left her to face alone their families and friends and neighbors without even an inkling as to why he had fled, felt remorseful. Never mind that he had treated her with such contempt. He imagined these words would be enough to make up for what he had done to her. After all this time.

She had not gone mad. He had.

Almost as if she stood outside herself, Jennet could measure the rage that had been building inside her, which presently rose so quickly it burned through every feeling, every thought, every particle of her being. Once a small, eternal ember of resentment, perhaps, now grew to the like of an inferno. She felt curiously in awe of such scalding, destroying emotion; she would surely burst into flame at any moment. Dimly she heard the clatter of her fan as it dropped from her hand.

She had nothing to say to him, but everything to do.

"Jenny, do not–" was all he got out before he ducked to avoid her fist.

Jennet would have tried to hit him again, but he seized her as he straightened, and dragged her up against him. That he dared have the audacity to put his hands on her and press her to him astounded her. He behaved as if they had remained in love and married and never wished to be parted from each other. As if she belonged to him.

"You will release me, sir," Jennet told the front of his shirt. "This instant."

"I knew this to be a mistake." He sounded as if he were talking to himself now. "I meant to keep my distance. I only thought… You have every right to hate me for what I did."

"Hate you?" she echoed as she looked up into his evil, beautiful green eyes. "I could kill you."

Greystone stared down at her as if she were a stranger. "Very nearly you did."

"I think I should remember if I had tried." Why could she not wrench herself away from him? He was holding her too tightly. "I wish to return to the ball." When he kept his hands on her she gritted her teeth. "Let go of me, Liam, or I will scream."

He did not let her go; indeed, he pressed her closer. Jennet could not bring her arms up to pummel him, so she opened her mouth and drew in a deep breath. In the next moment he covered it with his, muffling her shriek of fury with a kiss so carnal she should have fainted from the shock of being thus treated.

She would swoon later.

The night dissolved around Jennet as she clutched the rough fabric of his shirt, and then worked her hands up into his hair. Whoever had become Greystone no longer held her; this was Liam. The taste of him, the feel of his tongue, the heat of his breath mingling with hers, every part of the embrace hurled her back in time. Through the old silk of her costume she could feel his body hardening against hers, from the swell of his chest to the ridge of his manhood. Welcoming such desire made her own breasts pebble and ache, and her body soften as the onslaught of sensation radiated through her, snuffing out her wrath and replacing it with a need far more urgent.

Now she became his Jenny.

Greystone muttered something as he reached behind her, hefted her up against him and began to stride across the garden path. Jennet clung to him, hands and lips and legs, for she knew if she relinquished his kiss and took her hands from his long, thick mane she would collapse into a heap of ruin, never again to rise. Yes, this surely would end her, but such a glorious way to die.

Seven long, endless, barren years she had yearned for this.

She heard him yank open a door, sending a waft of warmer air over them both. She smelled flowers and greenery as he kicked the same door shut behind him. He swept his arm across something, and things rolled and shattered. He perched her on the cleared surface, and only then wrenched his mouth from hers.

Would he apologize again? If he did, she might truly have to take those gardening shears and stab him in his miserable heart.

Greystone regarded her for a long moment, and then his hands dropped between them. With one he gathered and tugged up her skirts and petticoats while the other busied itself with the front of his breeches. His movements, hurried yet graceful, silently attested to his familiarity with such activities. He meant to do what would be considered worse than abandoning her at the altar.

Fortunately there is no church filled with people to see your disgrace this time.

Jennet ignored the scathing whisper of her sensibility as she watched his eyes. His expression darkened as he exposed her legs, pushing the old silk up around her waist. It bemused her that he would apologize while intent on adding to her ruin— only this did not seem especially intentional.

No, Greystone appeared rather possessed by demons at present.

Knowing he would find no other hindrance beneath her skirts to bar him from having his way with her, Jennet knew the time had come to put an end to this. She must protest, scold him, plead with him, beg him to stop. Perhaps hit him again and bring him to his senses. Something had to at least be said. Why could she say nothing?

There is no more to say, her heart assured her, *and everything to do.*

In the end her body decided the matter. Jennet saw her hands reaching to help him, and felt the long, hard length of him come into her fingers. All iron swathed in thick satin, his cock swelled even larger as she caressed him. How splendid he was, all man, all wanting her. Nothing felt as good or right as shifting forward and parting her knees wide as she guided him to her slick, throbbing softness. The moment the heavy plum of his crown touched her he went rigid, and she curled her fingers around his shaft.

Greystone took firm hold of Jennet's throat, almost as if he meant to strangle her, and then slowly pressed into her body with his, his gaze locked with hers.

At first, he seemed too large to occupy such a small space, even with the abundance of wetness with which she engulfed him. A pang of distress tried to part the heavy, dragging craving she suffered, and then became of no consequence. Jennet felt herself stretching around him, her body trembling in response to this wholly unfamiliar possession, but this seemed the way of it. She had never taken a man into herself; of course, there would be newness to the accommodation. Her instincts told her this was where he was meant to be, and nature had fashioned her to accept him there.

Greystone's jaw tightened as he met resistance, something they both felt, and then it gave way with a brief yet startling, burning pain for Jennet. That soon faded as he pushed deeper, his hips moving in slow steadiness against her inner thighs, until he had joined their sexes entirely. Greystone dropped his hand and buried his face against her neck, his chest heaving as if he had just run to the village and back.

A curious tenderness filled Jennet, making sweeter the ache between her thighs.

Being thus penetrated, Jennet could also feel the beat of his heart ever so faintly inside her now. That pulsing made her clench around him, and she heard him groan against her neck. This pleased her, although she wasn't certain as to why. Her legs curled around the backs of his, and she braced herself with one hand on the table under her as she reached for his face. When her thumb brushed against the hard line of his mouth, he pressed his tongue against her palm.

Such a luscious thing to do, Jennet thought, her head filling with all manner of unseemly notions. She wished them away from the hot house, alone together in a bed chamber where they might be naked together on a soft bed. There she would ply her mouth on his flesh in a like fashion, from the curve of his lower lip to the arch of his feet and back again. She wanted him to move inside her for hours and hours, and satisfy this infernal craving for his flesh pumping inside her quim. She gasped as he plunged deeper, and the motion set all of her insides to heating and quivering. Again, and again he thrust into her, until she thought she should beg him to stop until she could catch her breath.

Breath lost its urgency as something rose from her belly and engulfed her breasts, her heart, her head. That incandescent bliss consumed her as anger never could, and Jennet surrendered to and triumphed over him, entirely lost, utterly found.

Greystone pressed her face against his shoulder, muffling her cries as he struggled to contain his groans. They rumbled against her breasts as he drove to the deepest realm of her core, and there held himself as his cock jerked and jetted, filling her with his seed. The satiny warm wetness mingled with her own, and when he drew away she nearly begged him to stay inside her, where he alone would ever belong, he alone would ever again be welcomed.

He kept one arm around her as he pressed a handkerchief between her thighs, and Jennet felt a glimmer of renewed arousal to watch him tend to her so gently. He then drew down her skirts, and attended to himself before fastening his breeches and stepping back from her, his eyes glittering with obvious gratification and no small amount of confusion. Carefully he took hold of her waist, and set her down on her feet.

Not a word had they spoken to each other since the kiss, Jennet thought absently. No expressions of affection, nor pledges of fidelity. An offer of marriage, she suspected, would not be forthcoming. He had taken what little she had kept from him, her innocence. He had done that so completely she would never again look upon any man as she once had.

No more to say, and now everything done.

Greystone might have spoken, had she waited and listened. Instead Jennet turned half toward the door, and then swung back, driving her fist directly into his face. This time she connected with his lordship's countenance, and with gratifying force. The pain for herself also proved significant, but it seemed a fair price for the pleasure of hearing and feeling her knuckles ram against his nose and mouth. He staggered backward and collided with a shelf of seedlings, sending them crashing to the floor.

Should she hit him again? Her hand throbbed painfully, but the rest of her felt magnificent. No, she had dealt with him properly.

Jennet walked out to retrieve her fan and her mask, donning the latter. She smoothed her hair, and shook out her skirts before she walked up to the doors to the reception room, and stepped inside.

From the windows overlooking the terrace Ruban watched the drama between Greystone and Jennet unfold. It brought back memories of another night recently spent in an old chateau, but not at a ball.

Jean-Pierre and his men had worked for three days on the traitor, who had been seen skulking from an officer's tent. By the time Ruban arrived the prisoner's features were no longer recognizable, and he bled from the ears as well as the nose and mouth.

"Without the cipher he could not read the messages," Ruban said after listening to their reports. "What else did you find on him?"

Jean-Pierre held up a small glass vial filled with a cloudy liquid. "Poison, we think. He tried to drink it after he was captured."

Such vials had been found on the bodies of other prisoners who had chosen death over torture. It had been whispered that all of them had been allies of the most ruthless, feared killer in France.

"I know you have met with the Raven," Ruban told the traitor, using a soothing tone. "Tell me his name."

The lie was one told to every captive in hopes of provoking a reaction, although it had not yet worked. This time the prisoner stiffened, and then looked away.

Being so close to finding the most hunted man in France made Ruban caress the battered face with real affection. "Tell me who he is, and where I may find him, and I will set you free."

"You cannot catch him," the traitor said, his tone taunting. "By now he is home in England."

"So, he is English." They had long suspected as much. "Where does he live there? London?" Ruban took out a dagger and showed it to the traitor. "Answer me, or I will make you beg for death—for weeks."

The prisoner lunged forward, impaling himself on the blade, and gurgled out a laugh before he died.

"Arrest this man's family, friends, and anyone who has been in his company," Ruban ordered the men. "By the time I arrive in London, I want to know where the Raven's home is."

In the end it had been the traitor's mistress who had confessed to seeing her lover write a message containing the words Renwick and Raven, which he had later handed off to another man in the streets of Paris. This startling information had been relayed to Ruban three days after the agent returned to England, but in the end the delay had helped more than hindered the search.

Now, had circumstances been slightly different, seeing Baron Greystone kiss and carry off Jennet Reed would have amused Ruban. Instead it proved yet another obstacle.

Still, the situation could be remedied.

Ruban slipped out of the house through

the door in the pantry where deliveries were brought in, and donned a matte black wool cloak before entering a tree grove across from the staircase tower. There Jean-Pierre stepped out from behind a wide trunk, his axe tucked into his belt and a pistol in each hand.

"I've changed the plan," Ruban told him. "As soon as the guests and the servants leave for the night, come in through the tower door. I will be waiting in the study."

"You cannot fool de Raven," Jean-Pierre pointed out, and gestured at Ruban's costume. "You stay behind, he know."

"We have yet to discover who the Raven is." Ruban thought for a moment, and then smiled. "But perhaps there is someone who already knows."

CHAPTER 10

Once he righted himself, Greystone brushed the potting soil from his costume and strode out of the hot house. He could see Jennet already inside the reception room, but she did not linger or look back at him. She disappeared from sight a moment later.

The fiery bliss he had experienced from taking her still hummed through his limbs, intensified by the pleasure he had given her in return. That she had remained a virgin all these years also gratified him, although he had no right to feel so smug about it.

Greystone had wondered too often about that since leaving her. Jennet was a beautiful woman, and unafraid of passion. He knew he had awakened her needs.

Although she had chosen never to marry, she might have discreetly taken a lover.

Why had she remained chaste? Surely not to save herself for him.

"You've done enough to the lass, milord," a hard voice said from behind him. "Let her go now."

He turned to see Pickering's man Foray standing at the corner of the hot house. The smug look on his homely face made Greystone's hands fist.

"You watched us, you bastard?" he demanded.

"No, but I've ears like a cat, and orders to patrol the grounds tonight." The valet cocked his head. "Couldn't find a way upstairs to a proper bed, then? Poor girl. Now I see why she tried to reshape your face."

The fact that Foray was right didn't soothe Greystone's temper. "Keep talking and I'll see to yours."

"Aye, I expect you would. Here." He tossed the sacking mask at him. "Pickering said you'd be riding out with him. You'll want a look at the nag."

After one last glance at the house,

Greystone turned and accompanied him through the gardens and out to the stables. Although everyone believed him to be nothing more than Pickering's manservant, Foray's particular talents had been learned as a street brat in the Devil's Acre. He had survived London's most notorious slum to join the Army, which had taught him even more lethal skills, and eventually found his way into Pickering's service. Foray had learned to dress his master as if he were Brummel himself, but he could also cripple a man with a single blow of the lead-filled sap he always carried.

He also knew that Greystone could easily do worse, and he'd never live to limp through his remaining years.

"I'd keep to the back roads until you reach Hackney," the valet said as he unlatched the stable door. "You'll be more likely to spot shadows. I've put two pistols in the satchel pack, but they'll be handier tucked in your belt."

Greystone disliked firearms; the blade or the garrote proved far more reliable. "Leave them."

In the stall stood a sturdy farm gelding,

with a saddle suitable to his role. Greystone checked over the mount before he adjusted the bridle to his liking. The animal was young and strong, and capable of the long ride ahead. As he stroked the mount he kept thinking of Jennet, and how her hands had felt on him. He should never have touched her. Worse, he wished nothing more than to return to the house, find her, and drag her to the nearest bed.

"You're not coming back to this wee corner of heaven, are you?" Foray asked idly. "Once it's finished, I mean."

Greystone eyed him.

"Just curious." The other man smiled, making his plain face look utterly menacing. "She's lovely–"

"–and much too good for me, as Pickering has already said." Despite knowing how deadly the valet was, Greystone felt tempted to test him. Then he understood his interest. "Are you questioning my loyalty? Arthur well knows that I burned down my life for this."

"Aye, and now you mean to take a torch to hers." As he took a step toward him the valet held up a broad hand. "Ever I've had a soft spot for the ladies."

Every word he spoke was true, and still Greystone wanted to beat him senseless. "Not that it is any of your concern, but Jennet Reed would have been my wife."

"You think she'd choose you again now?" The valet made a contemptuous sound. "It's not all swiving in the greenery, man. Women have expectations, and never more than after they've been duped. She'd want answers, and how would you explain why you left? Where you've been? What you've done? You can't, so you'd lie to her. Sharp as she is, she'd know it."

Jennet had never been able to read his intention to leave her, Greystone realized, because until the day before the wedding he hadn't planned to do anything but become her husband.

"You'd be the death of her, lad, or she yours," Foray said, almost kindly. "Be done with it."

He took in a deep breath and, with its release, let go of what few frustrations he could. "I will leave with your master as soon as the last of the guests depart." His jaw tightened, but he forced out the rest. "I will not be returning to Renwick."

Foray took a watch from his pocket, and opened it to check the time. "I'll put a man at her house for the next week, if it'll ease your mind."

"You'll do nothing of the sort," Greystone told him. "No one is to go anywhere near Miss Reed."

The valet regarded him for a long moment before he offered a mocking bow. "As you wish, milord."

CHAPTER 11

$\mathcal{A}$lthough he knew he should return to the ballroom to play host, Arthur Pickering first went to the second floor to make the rounds of the retiring rooms. It would not do for the vicar or his wife to walk in on any amorous young couple who had decided to make use of the available beds. He also had an uneasy feeling that refused to disperse.

The two rooms provided for the guests' needs happily remained empty, but a faint sound from down the hall drew Arthur to the closed door of his own bed chamber. He listened outside for a moment, and then opened the door and stepped in quickly.

Nothing but silence and shadows greeted him.

"Bloody old house." He went over to light a lamp on the night stand, but as soon as he did he saw a mound of old silk atop the coverlet on his bed.

Catherine Tindall lay on her side, watching him, as she held her loose bodice against her breasts. "You should not use such language in the presence of a lady, sir, especially one who is half-undressed."

"I beg your pardon, Miss Tindall." Arthur glanced down at the unlaced stays beside her on the bed. "Do you require assistance?"

"From you, sir?" She pouted her lips as she glanced at the ceiling. "Well, I can hardly go downstairs in this state."

He helped her off the bed, but as soon as she stood her bodice slipped down, revealing her pert breasts. He would have looked away, had she not cupped them with her dainty hands like two ripe fruits in offering.

"Do you like them?" Catherine asked. "They're rather large, I'm told. Larger than Jennet Reed's, certainly."

Her game became clear in an instant,

and Arthur turned his back on her. "That is not for me to say, Miss Tindall. I will go and find a lady to help you with your stays."

"I cannot breathe in them." Her arms came around him from behind, and she rubbed his belly with one and stroked his thigh with the other. Her skillful caresses attested to her familiarity with the male body. "I would much rather you help me out of this gown."

He turned around and took in a sharp breath, and smelled the mulled wine on hers. "You are drunk."

"A little, perhaps." Catherine plucked at his breech buttons. "Not enough to bring my father hammering on your door in the morning."

The Tindalls had great wealth and influence in London, Arthur knew. Catherine's father had the ear of the Regent, and her mother commanded near-equal respect as one of the most admired ladies among the town. To trifle with her would be exceedingly foolish. His cock, which now pushed at the fastening of his breeches, didn't care in the slightest.

Arthur pushed her back on the bed, jerking open his breeches as he watched her tug up her skirts. Beneath them she wore not a stitch, which laid her bare in the lamplight. She had even trimmed her nether hair in the shape of a heart, like a high-priced courtesan would.

"How rough you are, sir." Catherine smiled slowly as he produced the long shaft of his penis, and climbed atop her. "Well. You should show that more often when you are in society. Far more interesting than your dancing."

"While you enjoy playing the trollop in private." Arthur held himself just outside her gates and watched her squirm. "Or is that your true nature, and the giggling miss yet another mask you wear?"

"I am not laughing now," Catherine said, lifting her hips so that her sex caressed the swollen head of his.

Thrusting into her body made Arthur groan, for she felt as tight as a virgin. Yet the moment he possessed every inch of her warm, narrow channel she wriggled and began to squeeze him. She did so with the aplomb of a professional, so he allowed himself to take her as he pleased—hard and fast, with rude strokes that made her unable to hold him.

She did not find her pleasure, but seemed content to watch him have his.

Arthur jerked himself out of her before he spilled, painting her thighs with his seed. He then shifted to one side and put his fingers to her well-opened quim, stroking her deftly until she arched under his touch and squealed.

Stretching out on his back beside her, he turned his head to study her profile. He usually took more care with where he found his pleasure, but after the weeks of enforced celibacy the temptation had been too much to resist. He had not kissed her, which ladies of her set expected, nor had she offered her mouth. The only women he knew who had such a practical approach to intimacy made their living from it.

"Do you make a habit of such, er, spontaneity, my dear?" Arthur asked her.

"Of course not." Catherine reached over without looking and patted his chest as if to reassure him. "I have the benefit of a vastly experienced lover whom someday I will marry, Mr. Pickering. You may credit him with teaching me to fuck. We cannot meet often, however, or my parents would grow suspicious."

That sounded reasonable enough to him. "Since we have fucked, then, I believe you should call me Arthur."

"Why in heaven's name would I do that?" She slid herself off the bed and shook down her skirts. "People would make assumptions inconvenient to us both."

Arthur watched her peer into his mirror to replace and straighten her mask, and felt the blood rush back to his groin. "I should like to have you again before you go."

Catherine glanced back at him and fluttered her lashes. "Sir, you are insatiable." She came over to the bed, pushed him back flat, and opened his breeches. "Let me show you that which I most often employ to avoid other inconveniences. You will not have to spill on my legs this time."

His eyelids drooped as she curled her fingers around his hardening shaft, and brought the now-straining head to her lips.

"Your lover taught you to suck cock? I am all astonishment."

"That and more," she said just before she took him in her mouth, and slipped her fingers beneath his ballocks.

CHAPTER 12

The masquerade continued in boisterous fashion as Jennet joined those gathered in the ballroom. The music, the dancers and the laughter seemed overloud after the quiet gasps and carnal sounds she and Greystone had made in the hot house, but she did not mind. The noisier it was, the less opportunity she had to dwell on what she had done. Several gentlemen came to seek her as a partner, but she politely refused each one, claiming she had twisted her ankle. Instead she watched and listened and cursed herself silently.

Her family's reckless streak had finally emerged in her, it seemed, with a vengeance.

An odd memory of her mother sitting her down the night before her wedding came back to Jennet. Margaret had been red-faced and deeply embarrassed as she tried to explain what to expect once she and Liam were married. She'd used sparse and wholly inadequate terms for the act of marital bliss, as she called it.

Men have knowledge of such matters. You must trust in William to deal with you gently and kindly. There will be some small pain, perhaps, but only in the beginning part. If you are blessed, you will increase your family in two seasons, and give me a grandchild.

After their passionate embrace in the meadow Jennet had already guessed much of what to expect from Liam on their wedding night. The remaining facts she had deciphered long before that from her observation of animals on the estate. She also knew well the consequences of such acts for the female of any species. Now with the slight soreness throbbing between her thighs, she understood why the recollection had returned to her.

I could be with child.

"There you are, Miss Reed," a sweet

voice said. "I was hoping to bid you farewell, but Mr. Branwen has gone off somewhere, and well, may I sit with you until he returns for me?"

Jennet looked up at Deidre Branwen's hesitant smile, and tried to return it. "Of course, please do."

"Thank you." The vicar's wife arranged her full skirts as she perched on the chair beside her, and let out a sigh of relief. "I do envy the energy of the young. I have danced but twice and feel exhausted. You are far wiser than I."

"I doubt that, ma'am." This was her punishment for making love with Greystone, Jennet thought wryly: having to converse with the most good-hearted, moralistic woman in Renwick. "I hope all is well with you and the vicar."

"We are as tediously happy and content as ever." Deidre looked out at the dancers whirling to a merry waltz tune. "Lucetta and Harshad, my sister-in-law and her husband, will be coming to spend Christmas with us. I am counting the days now, for we have grown as close as true sisters. They bring their twins with them, such sweet boys. Do you know that Lucetta met Harshad here, at Dredthorne Hall?"

"No, I did not." Jennet had heard the gossip about the couple, of course; Lucetta Branwen had scandalized everyone in Renwick when she had married a gentleman from India. "Was it at a ball, like this one?"

"Oh, no, they both served the master here. That was a terrible time. We almost lost them to a madman, but I still cannot speak on that without weeping." The older woman's mouth thinned as she looked around them. "This place seems to draw tragedy to it. I would never have come, if not for my husband's insistence. He always wishes to be a constant presence in village society."

Jennet thought of all the times the vicar had come to Reed Park to look in on her and Margaret, especially after her mother had one of her panics. "He is a very good man, your husband."

"My father wished me to marry for wealth and position equal to that of our family." Deidre gave her a droll look. "You can imagine how he reacted when Mr.

Branwen asked for my hand. Who could be more unsuitable than a near-penniless curate? Yet despite all the obstacles I was quite determined, although not by any conscious, rational resolve. He claimed my heart the moment I first saw him."

As Liam had hers, Jennet thought. "Love at first sight, then. How romantic."

"I found it terribly inconvenient, and vexing, and confusing. Yet I never wavered. Eventually Papa had to agree, for I threatened to go to Scotland with Mr. Branwen." The older woman saw her reaction and patted her hand. "We believe we have some say regarding whom we love, but in truth I think love chooses us. We have but to decide if it is worthy of our devotion."

The vicar's wife was trying in her gentle way to warn her about Greystone, Jennet suspected, so she should set her mind at ease. "By chance does your husband have a younger, unattached brother?"

Deidre shook her head and laughed.

"Jennet, there you are." Catherine appeared in front of them, her cheeks flushed and her eyes bright. "Hello, Mrs.

Branwen. You are the patron saint of sheep tonight." She frowned. "There is a saint of sheep, is there not?"

"Oh, yes. Saint George of Lydda," Deidre said, rising from her chair. "Excuse me, my dears. The hour is growing late, and I must find my husband." She smiled at Jennet and then made her way past the dancers.

"This is such fun," Catherine told her, dropping down into the chair the vicar's wife had vacated. She patted down the ballooning flounce of her skirts before she said, "I have danced and danced and danced again. London has nothing on the country."

Her friend's inelegant perch and slurred voice surprised Jennet, as did the smell of male sweat coming from her. "I thought you would stay with the cider tonight."

"You know how much I hate the taste of apples. The wine is far superior." She glanced down at the empty goblet in her hand, and then peered at Jennet. "Why do you sit here like a lump? I must see you enjoy yourself. Allow me to find a partner for you."

Jennet caught her hand as Catherine started to rise, and then had to catch her as she reeled. "I think the time for you to go home has arrived, my dear."

"Truly?" Her friend made a face and pressed a hand to her brow. "Oh, dear. Perhaps I should. Presently my head wishes to waltz by itself."

Putting an arm around her, Jennet walked her from the ballroom out to the front entry, where she had the footman summon her carriage. When it arrived, she walked the very unsteady Catherine out and helped her inside.

"Why do you stand out there?" her friend asked. "Get in."

"I must speak to Mr. Pickering before I leave." That was a lie, but she needed more time to collect herself before she returned home. Fortunately, many of her neighbors remained in attendance; she would beg a ride to Reed Park from one of them. "I will call on you tomorrow afternoon to return the gown. Good-night."

"Your dear mama will be very cross with me," Catherine predicted, and then almost fell over as the carriage started down the drive.

CHAPTER 13

Greystone heard someone approaching the stables and looked out expecting to see Foray or Pickering. Instead a short gentleman dressed as a humble shepherd came to the doors. When he stepped out the man seemed unsurprised to see him.

"Mr. Gerard, I– Forgive me, Baron Greystone," the shepherd said, his pleasant tenor giving away his identity. He bowed and added, "When I inquired, our host said that I might find you here."

"Mr. Branwen." Suspecting Pickering was having another joke at his expense. He returned the bow. "How may I be of service?"

"I should like to have a word with you

before I leave for the night. I confess that my wife and I do not keep late hours." He removed his mask and turned it in his hands. "For that reason, I promise to be brief. It is about Miss Reed."

Greystone suddenly had the sense of being a boy about to be scolded.

"As it happens I spoke with her earlier about you." Jeffrey's brow furrowed. "I worried she might be in some distress over the possibility of meeting you again. That is presumptuous, I admit, but as she has no father to watch over her, I feel somewhat obligated."

"Miss Reed and I did meet earlier." He resisted touching his still-throbbing nose. "I believe everything between us has been settled amicably."

"I would take your word for that, of course, had I not witnessed your meeting Miss Reed earlier." He made a surprisingly savage gesture in the general direction of the gardens. "You kissed her, and then you carried her off. I saw it all from the window."

Greystone rubbed his brow. "Mr. Branwen, I can appreciate your concern—"

"You cannot possibly, sir." The little vicar squared his shoulders as if preparing for a fight.

"–but this is none of your business," he finished before he thought better of it.

"On the contrary, my lord. You made it mine long before tonight." Jeffrey marched up to him and poked a finger at his chest. "You did not come to the church at the appointed hour for your wedding. You offered no warning, or explanation, or apology. You vanished without a word to anyone. By doing so you broke a solemn promise you made, not only to Miss Reed, but to God. You were not there to see the consequences. I was. I have been, these seven years."

What could he say in his defense? Nothing, thanks to the other solemn promise he had made.

The vicar stepped back and visibly tried to compose himself. "Forgive me. I rarely lose my temper, but when I do my ability to minister to others suffers."

"What have you said that I do not deserve?" Greystone asked. "I am sorry that I upset you, Mr. Branwen. I will be gone from here tonight, and I have no plans to return."

"If there are consequences for Miss Reed after tonight, you will," Jeffrey said flatly. "You will come back to Renwick and do right by that young woman. You will stand up with her in my church, before God, and marry her." He leaned closer, his gaze intent. "And if I must travel to London to drag you back here to do so, sir, rest assured I will."

Consequences.

Greystone watched as Jeffrey turned and stalked back to the house. Only when he was out of earshot did he slump back against the stable wall and close his eyes. He had not given a single thought to what might result from making love to Jennet. The moment he had kissed her he had been consumed by his passion for her. Nothing had mattered but her. The world might have crumbled around them, and he wouldn't have noticed.

Now she might be carrying his child, doomed to be born out of wedlock in a small village where everyone would revile and shun them both.

He would marry her, Greystone decided. As long as she had his name Jennet would be protected. She could live at Gerard Lodge with the child and her mother. He would see to it that they wanted for nothing. Once his own mother learned Jennet was his wife, and with child, she would likely wish to join them. They could be happy together, the three of them, raising his heir. Staying away would not be difficult. Men were never much help in the nursery. He would have the consolation of knowing he had saved her and their baby from the very worst of scandals.

It was all decided, except for one problem. The thought of not being with Jennet while she grew heavy with his child made Greystone want to howl at the heavens until the sky splintered and the stars rained down.

Remember your choice.

JENNET RETURNED INSIDE, where she stood for a long moment eyeing the empty reception room. If she sat there no doubt

Greystone would find her; if she went to the ballroom he might have the audacity to ask her to dance. She needed a quiet place to tidy herself and think, and recalled what the older woman had said after they had first arrived.

Taking the stairs to the second floor, Jennet kept watch for other guests, but found herself alone when she walked out from the landing. She saw several doors standing open as if in invitation, and looked in the one nearest the stairs before entering the room.

The bed chamber inside had a curious mix of antique oak furnishings and new golden linens and ivory damask drapes. Fresh paint and plaster repairs failed to entirely disguise the cracks and chips in the walls, just as the new carpet only covered most of the scarred floor planks. Some landscape paintings had been hung, and a low fire burned in the hearth, but Jennet doubted Arthur Pickering or any of his friends currently occupied the chamber. So why did she feel as if someone were watching her from inside the room?

"Forgive my intrusion," Jennet said, loud

enough to be heard in the adjoining dressing room. When no one replied, she closed the door and went to the wash stand.

Even as she made liberal use of the soap and cold water, she could still smell Greystone's scent. She would have to scrub every vestige of him from her person in the morning; for now, she tidied herself as best she could. Additional measures would have to be taken with the borrowed gown. She would sponge the silk with spirits mixed with a little honey and vinegar, and let it dry in the shade out of doors to remove any lingering trace of her assignation in the hot house. The rest of her garments she could rinse out in her bath water.

Greystone would not have to do any of that, nor wait for weeks to discover if he was with child. That made Jennet hate him just a little more.

Once she had finished the necessities, she sat down by the fire to think. What she had done in the hot house with Greystone could be concealed; a pregnancy could not. Every woman knew the disastrous consequences of having a child out of wedlock. Bearing his child while yet unmarried would earn Jennet the contempt of the world. It would horrify her mother, scandalize their servants, and estrange every friend they had.

I have been so foolish.

Not only would she be cast out of society, and never again be permitted to rejoin it, but the baby and Margaret would share the same fate. Jennet's name would be spoken of only as a warning to other young ladies, and then only in whispers. The Reeds would remain in social exile for the remainder of their lives, and her child would be evermore known as Greystone's bastard.

Despite these dismal thoughts her hand crept down to touch the top of her skirt, and a strange warmth suffused her.

Never had Jennet dared dream of becoming a mother, but the prospect served to strengthen her resolve. Greystone would not care about the baby any more than her, but with some careful arrangement she could bear it without destroying her or Margaret's reputation. She had heard stories of girls who went away to Scotland or Ireland to have a secret confinement, and returned a year or two later wearing wedding rings and pretending to be widows while presenting their infants. Everyone suspected the truth of such matters, but accepted the pretense.

Would she be bold enough to try the same?

The hope she felt soothed her, and she closed her eyes for a moment. That moment stretched out as she fell into a doze, and then into a dream.

Jennet found herself standing in a cemetery, her costume now covered with black feathers. Before her gaped a deep rectangular hole in the ground framed by four long, sharp-looking scythes. She took a step back, and then leaned forward to look into the grave, which thankfully proved empty. A black marble headstone had been placed at one end, but dozens of names had been chiseled into its surface.

All of them ended with the same surname: Thorne.

"I should like to awaken now," Jennet said, removing the velvet mask from her face. The fabric had turned black, and fell apart in her hands, fluttering to the ground to become more gleaming dark plumes.

"You are in no immediate peril, my dear," a deep voice said. "Yet I think you must awaken very soon."

She turned toward the other end of the grave, where stood a tall, heavy-set older man wearing clothes from a century past. A powdered wig sat somewhat askew on his head, which he absently adjusted as he gazed down into the grave. That he was partly transparent and floated slightly above the ground made it obvious he was some form of apparition.

Jennet blinked, but he did not vanish. "I beg your pardon, sir?"

"On the best of days Dredthorne Hall is a precarious place, my dear," the old man told her. "This is All Hallows' Eve. Tonight, every soul lost within these rooms has been awakened. Most intend only to wander, but among them walk malevolent and vengeful spirits that one should not cross."

"I do not believe in ghosts or spirits," Jennet told him. "Nor have we been introduced. Pray, what is your name?"

"Forgive my discourtesy." The man bowed. "I am Emerson Thorne."

"You are the gentleman who built Dredthorne Hall?" When he nodded, she belatedly remembered to curtsey. "Of course, I must be dreaming."

"You have a gift of seeing what others do not," Thorne told her. "Even in your sleep, I would wager. I am sorry to say that ladies with your talent do not fare well in my house."

Jennet smiled politely. "I am imagining you, sir, so I have no need for your reassurance."

The cemetery became flooded with shadows, which whirled around them before receding. She found herself walking through the gardens, the ghost of Emerson Thorne floating beside her. All around them sprang flowers and vines and leaves made of ice and frost, which sparkled in the bright moonlight. The dazzling radiance made her squint until she spied other diaphanous silhouettes moving along the pathways. All of them appeared to be ladies, each dressed in gowns from the last century.

When they noticed Jennet and Thorne, they flew back into the hall, passing directly through the stone walls.

"If you are indeed haunting Dredthorne, what keeps you here?" she asked Thorne.

"Before I built my home, there stood on these grounds the ruins of an ancient fortress. It fell during the invasion of William the Conqueror. Many hundreds of Saxons died here, where I built my dream home." The old man sighed. "I should have respected the dead, but I was in love and had not a thought for anyone but my lady. I had the ruins cleared, and Dredthorne built. My rival murdered my wife here. Many other Thorne wives were killed, or driven mad."

His rambling sounded like the stuff of delusions, but Jennet felt a sudden welling of dread. "I am not married to a Thorne, or any man, for that matter."

Thorne chuckled sadly. "My family has many branches, including a very distant connection to the Gerard family. Midnight has passed, so you have spent the night in my house, and made yourself William's wife in everything but name."

Jennet wanted to laugh it off as part of this ridiculous dream, but in her heart she felt the truth of what he had said. "What would you have me do, sir?"

"Use your gift to your advantage," the old man said sternly. "If you are clever, I think you may live to see the morning."

"What am I to look for, Mr. Thorne?" As he started to float back to the house, Jennet reached out without thinking and touched the sleeve of his jacket. Her hand passed through it, and when she snatched it back it felt as cold as if it were encased in ice.

"What they cannot see, Miss Reed." Thorne glanced back at her. "An end to the curse on Dredthorne Hall. You must be the one to break it."

ONCE THE LAST of the guests had left, Pickering paid and dismissed the servants for the night. The speed with which his temporary staff left amused him, for he didn't share their fear of the old house. Dredthorne Hall had the sort of shabby, pathetic charm possessed by an aging

French courtesan who refused to surrender to the ravages of time. One had to admire that sort of tenacity.

Catherine Tindall had surprised him, a rare experience. He had enjoyed burying himself in the soft vise of her quim, and plumbing the warm, wet paradise of her lips. He wasn't too certain if he cared for the other things she had done while fellating him, but the entire interlude had been refreshingly novel. Perhaps when she returned to the city he would make a point of calling on her, and arrange another tryst.

His smile faded as he considered the task ahead. He and Greystone would ride until dawn to reach London, where he would deliver the goods and then report to his superiors. His recommendations would not be welcome, but after seeing the baron's reaction to Jennet Reed, he could no longer be relied upon as expected. Indeed, he felt certain that if William returned to his work, he might expose them all.

Pickering entered the study to retrieve his satchel, and heard the door slam shut behind him. He glanced over his shoulder expecting to see Foray or Greystone, and looked into the dark, flat eyes of a killer.

Unwelcome as they were, it seemed his last guests had arrived.

"I say, the ball is over, dear chap." After noting the knife scars on the intruder's hands, he started for his desk, only to find another brute blocking his path. "You gentlemen should finish out the night at the village tavern. The wine tastes little better than swill, but their ale proves surprisingly good." He waggled his brows. "The little blonde at the taps is even better."

"Sit down," the one with the scars growled, his English as thick as his muscles. "Ruban comes to speak with you."

Pickering feigned a puzzled look as he did as he was told, but a chill collected in his chest. He knew Ruban's reputation to be well-earned, and his own limited skills useless in this situation. He would never again leave this room alive. Since he had long ago accepted that as a very possible fate, that left tending to matters to protect those who might survive the night.

Everything depended on Greystone now.

Oddly Pickering thought of Jennet Reed, and the sharpness in her lovely eyes. Since he preferred skillful whores to ladies, and remaining unencumbered rather than playing the devoted husband, Pickering felt few regrets. He wasn't sorry he had bedded her friend, but he regretted his pretense of pursuing Jennet. She was a true lady, and her heart still belonged to another. He found himself simply wishing he could see her smile one last time, and hear that delightful laugh of hers. Of all the women he had ever admired, she was the most superb.

He also had to put an end to this farce before Ruban arrived to question him, so he turned his thoughts to his duty. The henchmen guarding him seemed nervous, and not particularly clever. He had encountered many such men in his time, and knew exactly how to provoke them.

"I think there has been a terrible mistake." Casually he picked up a file containing the deeds to Dredthorne. "I do have something that may be of interest to your emperor, however. If I give it to you, will you spare my life?"

The scarred agent smiled, showing too many teeth. "But of course."

Pickering stood and came around the desk, doing his best to appear hopeful and eager. As soon as he drew near the hearth he flung the file into it, setting it aflame. The big brute snatched at it, and the other men shouted. He smiled even as he felt the blade hit him and bury itself in his back. Tottering a little, he returned to his desk, and with the last of his strength sat down.

"What did you do?" the brute demanded as he loomed over him.

"Why, I won, you idiot." As the darkness crowded close, Pickering closed his eyes, and let it take him.

CHAPTER 14

What brought Jennet out of her peculiar dream was the smell of her former betrothed and one-time lover. As she sat up his scent seemed to grow even more pronounced, and she turned her head to find it coming from the upholstery. At some point this night he must have sat in the same spot to leave his scent there.

Had she come to his room without even realizing it? Or had he come in while she had been dozing? Was he standing somewhere in the shadows, watching her?

Jennet allowed her stiffened shoulders to relax, and made a show of yawning and stretching. As she did so her gaze wandered around the chamber, but once more there seemed to be nothing to indicate any presence other than her own. She heard nothing but a distant creaking sound, likely from the wind against the old shutters. What she did see was the narrow door to the balcony standing a little ajar. Rising as silently as she could, she tiptoed over to it, took hold of the knob, and yanked it open.

The balcony stood empty.

"You are being a ninny," Jennet told herself as she stepped out onto the veranda. The wind had grown lighter but colder, and beneath her she could see Prudence Hardiwick and two other young ladies climbing into a carriage. The rig in front of them held two gentlemen who were laughing and calling back to the ladies something about being the last to go. They looked as if they had imbibed just as much as Catherine.

Catherine.

Jennet called out and waved to them in hopes of stopping them. By that time both parties were driving off, however, and the clatter of horse hooves on the drive drowned out her voice. Hoping to catch them, she hurried out of the chamber and down the stairs, but by the time she reached the front entry the drive stood empty. As she turned she saw the footmen had also gone, likely to clean up after the guests. She went directly to the ballroom, which stood empty.

"Hello?" Jennet felt slightly alarmed now. "Is anyone here?"

A low moaning sound came in from the adjoining room, but when she stepped out to see who made it, she found herself facing the black cat that had earlier darted across the drive. The feline regarded her with its yellow-green eyes for a moment before it padded over to rub itself against her skirts.

"This is the second time you have crossed my path tonight," Jennet told it sternly, and then sighed and crouched down to pet it. "Never mind me. I do not believe you leave bad luck behind in your travels. If Mama would not break out in a rash the moment she beheld you, I would take you home with me."

The cat purred loudly and pushed its head against her fingers, and then went oddly still. It swung its head toward a painting hanging above the mantel across from them, and then just as suddenly scampered out.

Jennet regarded the portrait, which showed an older man sitting on a wooden bench surrounded by a patch of roses. He appeared to be staring off at something with great affection, judging by the smile on his mouth. She walked over, and to her astonishment she realized that his face matched that of the man from her dream.

The etched brass plate at the bottom of the frame read Emerson Thorne at Dredthorne, 1714.

Slowly she backed away from the portrait, but she couldn't look away from the eyes, which seemed now to be watching her.

"I must have seen it when I came into the ballroom earlier," Jennet muttered, although all she could recall was feeling furious and foolish at the same time. "I do not believe in ghosts. There is no curse, either."

As if Thorne had heard her, he spoke from her memory. *You must be the one to break it.*

A low yowl made Jennet flinch, and she

looked over to see the black cat again, this time standing with its back arched in front of an open door. Hurrying over to it, she looked in and let out a sigh of relief as she saw it was a study. Arthur Pickering sat behind the desk by the window, his head resting against the cushions, his eyes closed.

He looked as exhausted as she felt.

"Mr. Pickering, I am so happy to find you." Jennet stood in the doorway, and waited for his reply. He didn't stir, so she kept talking as she entered the study. "I fell asleep in one of the chambers upstairs, and now I seem to be stranded. I was hoping to return home with one of my neighbors. Perhaps I could prevail on you to call for your carriage?"

Pickering said nothing, and would not look at her.

"I am very sorry to wake you, but I cannot spend the whole night here. Mr. Pickering?" She reached to touch his shoulder, and then froze as he slumped forward against the desk. The hilt of a dagger protruded from the back of his blood-soaked jacket, assuring her that he would never again answer her or anyone.

* * *

GREYSTONE WATCHED from the stables as the last carriages left Dredthorne Hall. He'd felt it prudent to remain away from the house until everyone had left, and Jennet with them. Now he could go about his work without complication or distraction. She would hate him the more now for taking advantage of her before he left again. He would have preferred to have more than one wild embrace in the wildflowers to remember on cold, lonely nights.

All was as it should be.

As he approached the door to the staircase tower that led into the kitchens, Greystone caught the faintest trace of a particular, alarming odor coming from the firewood bin. He knew the stench too well to mistake it, but went to carefully lift the lid and look inside.

Foray lay among the splits, his eyes wide as he stared sightlessly at him. Blood from a deep gash across his throat covered the front of him.

Greystone closed his eyes, and lowered the lid carefully to avoid making any more sound. He then turned to scan the immediate area. More blood stained the ground where he suspected the valet had been ambushed; from the scuffling marks in the dirt he had tried to fight free before his throat had been cut. From there his body had been dragged to the bin. Two sets of boot prints, one small and one large, led into the house. When he bent down to peer closely at them he saw traces of Foray's blood, which they both had stepped in.

Greystone recognized their method. One had approached to distract Foray long enough for the other to come from behind to attack. He straightened and listened for any sound of movement around him. The assassins had killed Foray to enter the house and move against Pickering and the two guards he had brought with him from London.

When they didn't get what they wanted, they would kill them all.

He reached down to take the dagger from his boot, and walked silently around to the back of the hall. Lights still flickered in most of the windows, giving him a partial view of each room beyond them. All of the footmen had vanished from their posts, and he saw no sign of any of his colleagues, either. One of the garden doors to the reception room had been left open, and through that he heard two low voices arguing in French.

"Oú est-il?" *Where is he?*

"Je le retrouverai. Emporte la fille." *I will find him. Grab the girl.*

Greystone heard something rustle behind him, but as he turned something heavy slammed into his head, hurling him into the black.

* * *

JENNET STEPPED BACK from Pickering's body, her heart pounding so loudly she could hear it inside her head. For once she understood why her mother became so distraught in moments of panic. She could happily scream herself hoarse, or faint where she stood. Possibly both.

A man is dead. Now is not the time to become Margaret.

Slowly her reason reasserted itself and coaxed her away from the edge of hysteria.

She must make some sense of this. Pickering could not have stabbed himself in the back; someone murdered him. They had also arranged his body so that he would appear asleep.

Was he truly dead?

Jennet inched closer, and pressed her fingers to his neck, just beneath his jaw. She felt no heartbeat, and his flesh had already gone cool and stiff. Touching him made her want to shudder, but then she saw the set of his mouth. He looked almost as if he were gratified, as if he had won some final skirmish before dying.

"I am so sorry this happened," Jennet murmured.

At that moment the fortune-teller's words came back to her: Before this dance is done, you will see your own death.

"The dance is over," she told herself, although looking at the knife in Pickering's back made goosebumps rise on her skin. Whoever had murdered him might still be hiding somewhere in the house—but who would wish him dead, and why?

Jennet noticed traces of soot blackened his sleeves, and now she could smell the faintest odor of smoke coming from him. Glancing at the hearth, she saw a fragment of singed paper on the bricks, and paper ash among the glowing coals. He had burned something, but why?

"Be at peace, sir." She moved her hand to his cheek for a moment before she turned and called out as loudly as she could, "Hello, is someone there? Please, I need help in the study. Please come quickly."

Jennet heard footsteps, and hurried to the door. There she nearly collided with three men dressed in heavy coats and hats, and wearing black masks over their faces. For a moment she thought they might be guests who had lingered, until she saw their eyes, and the pistols in their hands. She spun and ran for the window behind the desk, but before she reached it hard hands grabbed her and dragged her back. She fought, screaming as she tried to wrench free.

One of the men jerked her around and slapped her so hard she would have fallen if not for the other two seizing her arms.

"Enfermez-la," the brute said to the others, who dragged her out of the study.

Jennet understood French well enough to know they had been ordered to lock her away. This seemed the perfect moment for a swoon, which she feigned at once. They lifted her off her feet and carried her between them through the house, unaware that she kept her eyes open to slits and watched everything they passed until they entered the dining room.

They brought her to the back wall, where one of them inserted a key into a slot in the painted panel. The wall swung out like a door, and they carried her inside and dropped her before leaving. She didn't move until she heard them turning the lock, and then cautiously lifted her head.

Moonlight from a window provided some thin light on the small room, which appeared to be a library of sorts. A series of mirrored panels occupied one side of the room, but shelves covered the other walls. From the dusty state of the books Jennet doubted that anyone had used the concealed library in years.

She couldn't see any candles or lamps about, and only ashes filled the old hearth to one side. As she pushed herself upright,

Jennet's hand touched what felt like a sleeve. She squinted until she made out the silhouette of a man sprawled on his back.

"Sir?" Surely he had to be one of the servants who had been similarly assaulted by the brutes. Yet when she moved to lean over him she saw that a scar divided one of his brows, and the silver hair at his temples. "Oh, my God, no. Liam."

Greystone did not stir.

Terrified now, she touched his neck with a shaking hand, and uttered a small cry of relief when she felt his pulse throbbing beneath his warm skin. He was not dead. They had not murdered him. His chest barely moved, however, and when she slid her hand to his cheek she felt the sticky warmth of blood. A new rage bloomed in her breast, but she clamped down on it. She had to think rationally, and make use of her resources.

She needed him more than anything.

"You must awaken now, my lord." Jennet patted his cheek, but he remained unmoving. "Baron Greystone, we have been taken captive, and Mr. Pickering murdered. You must help me."

Still he did not stir, and she began to fear the worst. Had he been stabbed as well? Would she find a dagger in his back, and blood pouring out of him? How could she go on if he died in her arms?

An unreasonable anger rose up inside her, and she shook him.

"You cannot die, Liam. No matter how often in the past I've wished you dead, this night I absolutely forbid it." She took hold of his shoulders, pushing him over until she could see his back. When she didn't see a knife, she rolled him to his back and then shook him as hard as she could manage.

A low groan came from his chest, and his shoulders moved under her hands.

No one would have blamed Jennet for what she did next. She dropped down on him, plastering herself against his chest, and held onto him as she fought back her sobs. He would not die, not in this house, not tonight. They would work together and find a way out of this.

Once she had regained her control, Jennet pushed herself upright.

"I need your help, my lord. Doubtless you have survived worse," she added, grimacing as she tried to pull him into a sitting position. "That scar above your eye attests to your fortitude as well as your foolishness. We will need more of the former if we are to see the dawn." She was babbling, but considering what she had endured, she was entitled. "Come now. Look at me. Show me you have regained some of your senses."

"Jenny." He opened one eye and peered at her. "What the devil?"

"Arthur Pickering has been murdered," she told him. "I found his body in the study. Someone stabbed him in the back. He was burning something, I think. When I called for the servants to help me, three masked men seized and dragged me here. They spoke French. Did they attack you?"

"Yes, outside." Greystone turned his head. "Where are we?"

"I believe it is Dredthorne Hall's much-lauded hidden library." She nodded toward the door. "We have been locked in."

"Of course, we have." He closed his eyes for a moment. "For God's sake, why did you stay? You should have left with the others."

"I fell asleep upstairs." Was he going to

blame her for their predicament? "By the time I awoke everyone had gone. Why are you still here?"

Greystone rose with slightly unsteady movements, examining the room around them before he went and listened at the door. He returned to help her up and looked all over her.

"Did they harm you?" When she shook her head, he turned her toward the window and touched her swollen cheek, his fingers gentle. "And this?"

"When they seized me, they did not care for my screaming. It is nothing." She fought an urge to rub her face against his hand. "Truly, my lord, I am well."

"I will attend to whoever struck you, I promise," Greystone said, sounding almost eerily calm as he reached under his shirt and unstrapped something, removing a thin dark case. "What did these men say to you?"

"Nothing at all. One spoke in French to the others, and told them to lock me up. They all seemed genuinely menacing. Do you think they meant to rob Mr. Pickering? Why would they be French?" She watched as he took what appeared to be a long metal instrument from the case. "What is that?"

"A tool." He walked over to the door, listened again, and then inserted the lock pick into the key hole. "You are quite certain that Arthur was dead?"

"He had a knife in his back, and did not breathe or move. I could not find a pulse on his neck." Jennet joined him at the door and watched as he carefully turned the pick. "How can you do this?"

"It is part of my work." He met her gaze. "To serve the crown in my position, such skills are required."

Jennet frowned. "You are His Majesty's locksmith?"

"That is one way of putting it." Greystone turned his attention back to the lock. "How many men did you see in total?"

"Only the three who grabbed me. You are a gentleman, and heir to a great estate, but you have employment? Why would you need to work?" When he didn't reply she folded her arms. "Did your father gamble away all of his fortune? Or did you? Oh, Liam. Tell me you did not."

"It was never about money." He cursed

under his breath before he added, "I pose as a French merchant supplying the emperor's soldiers."

"You would have to do that…in France." When he nodded, bile rose in her throat, making it hard to speak. "Exactly which crown do you serve in your capacity, my lord?"

"Ours, my dear. I am their spy." Something clicked, and he drew the pick out from the lock. He tried the door, frowned and then reinserted the instrument. "The locks in this house are newer than those I have encountered in my travels, and I am not particularly adept at this. It will take some time."

Nothing he said made any sense to her. "Very good, then while you work you can explain to me how you became a spy."

"Without His Majesty's permission, I cannot. The work is very sensitive." Greystone shifted as the lock made a rusty sound. "There, I almost have it."

Jennet felt her stomach knot and leaned back against the wall. "This is why you would not marry me? Because you wished to play-act a merchant while you wander about the French countryside spying?"

"More I cannot tell you," he said, sounding tired now. "Only know that my leaving had nothing to do with you."

"Oh, of course it didn't," she said, making a careless gesture. "We were only to be married, that morning. I cannot imagine why I should be involved in your decision. I was to be your wife. No one of importance at all."

He sighed. "I meant only that you played no part in the decision."

Greystone assumed the length of their parting had made her memories of him fade. Even now she could see the twitch of the muscle along his jaw, the tension in his shoulders and the fact that he would not look directly at her.

"Do you think you can lie to me like this and I would not know?" Jennet demanded. "You, a spy. I would sooner believe my mother a witch. Have the decency to admit that you left me in pursuit of your own desires, whatever in God's name they were. Go on. I will not faint. I did not faint on the day you left, as it happens."

He eyed her. "What did you do?"

"I brought Mama home, and went to my room, and much more than that I cannot remember. I tore my wedding gown to shreds and had Mrs. Holloway burn the remains," she tacked on. "What did you do? Oh, of course, you cannot tell me. It is spy business."

"I left behind everything I wanted that day." Greystone hesitated before he added, "Indeed, I think the only pleasure I have felt since I left Renwick was with you in the hot house tonight."

She turned her back on him. "Do not remind me of how shamelessly I behaved."

"You did nothing wrong," he said softly. "The blame is mine. I seduced you."

"Given how practiced you are at such endeavors, I should not disagree, but we both wished it to happen." Jennet rubbed her eyes. "I knew you would be here tonight. I knew I should never come. Yet here I am, and now disgraced again. No matter what I do, it seems to be my fate."

Greystone smiled a little. "Was it so terrible to make love with me, Jenny?"

Answering that would require honesty

on her part that she had no intention of offering to him. "Being an unmarried lady, I have nothing to compare to the experience."

"I regret that I hurt you. I had thought…" He stopped and sighed. "I would not have touched you, had I known it to be your first time with a man."

How glad she was that only the moon provided light now, for her face felt as if it were flaming—but not with embarrassment.

"You mean that you assumed that I took lovers after you abandoned me?" Jennet demanded, newly outraged. "Or that I married someone else? Well, sir, I did neither thing. I am the same as I was when you left Renwick. Or I was, until this night's madness." She rubbed her brow. "I cannot believe I am going to say this, but my mother was right."

The lock chose at that moment to make an odd, metallic screech, and the door creaked as it swung inward. Greystone opened and held it as he peered through the gap, and then turned to her.

"You must not make a sound," he warned.

CHAPTER 15

After returning to the parsonage, Deidre Branwen retreated to her dressing room to remove her shepherdess costume and don her nightdress. She did so with relief, for she had never liked pretense of any sort. She also felt deeply disquieted by their visit to Dredthorne Hall. Jeffrey had claimed it perfect, as it had been years since anyone had come to harm there, and that was likely true. Still, from the moment they had entered the old house Deidre had felt very nervous. For all the lamps and candles, too many shadows filled the rooms, as if shades of those who had died there lurked in the corners, watching for the next lost soul to join them.

"You are being mutton-headed again," Deidre told her reflection.

As she brushed out and braided her hair, she expected to hear Jeffrey enter their bed chamber to begin his nightly ablutions, but the adjoining room remained oddly quiet. Her husband had been equally silent during their carriage ride home from Dredthorne Hall, his expression distant as he stared out the window.

Something had happened during the brief time when he had left her in the ball room, Deidre suspected. Whatever that was, he had also brought it home with him.

Quickly she washed her face before going in search of him. Their sitting room remained dark, as did the kitchen, so she went down the hall to Jeffrey's study. He had left the door open, yet when she looked in he was not sitting at his desk. Instead he stood before the portrait of Thomas More, his hands clasped behind his back as he stared at the martyr.

"Do not leave, my dear," Jeffrey said when Deidre would have crept away. "I had hoped gazing upon Saint Thomas would provide me with some solace, but that silly scholar's cap he wears continues to distract me."

His attempt at humor did not mask the agitation in his voice, which drew her to his side. She tucked her hand in his as she studied the painting of his personal hero. Jeffrey never dwelled on the man's persecution of Protestants, which she personally considered a ghastly business. Yet he had been a man of his time, and his religious conviction could not be denied. He had refused to abandon his beliefs, and had sacrificed his life for his faith.

"It is his nose for me," Deidre said. "Very large, I must say. That ridge between his brows, just above the bridge, my father had one of those from frowning excessively. What has upset you, my love?"

"Tonight, I spoke to William Gerard." The admission came out of him accompanied by a heavy sigh. "Baron Greystone, I should say. I confronted him about his behavior toward Miss Reed, lost my temper and threatened to do him bodily harm. I think if he had said the wrong thing to me, I would have."

"My dear, that was so long ago," she

couldn't help reminding him. "What good does it now to chastise the man?"

"I witnessed William compromising Jennet tonight." Jeffrey rubbed his brow. "I did not wish to. It was purely by accident that I did. From what I saw she welcomed his attentions, and his were quite enthusiastic. I daresay they still love each other. Yet later I found him in the stables with a saddled horse behind him. I believe he means to abandon her again."

"How awful." Deidre recalled the light pink marks she had seen on Jennet's neck and cheek in the ball room; the unmistakable signs left by a passionate embrace. "Do you imagine she may have, ah, sprained her ankle?"

They often used such euphemisms for the most intimate of situations; that was their reference for a lady who had gotten with child out of wedlock.

"I cannot tell you now, but by next summer we should know." He made a disgusted sound. "I am angrier with myself than anyone. I should have put a stop to it, and taken her from that rogue." He gestured toward the portrait. "As Saint Thomas believed, *qui tacet consentire videtur*, one who does nothing may as well consent."

"If that is your thinking, then you would be complicit in every wrong done in this parish, I should think." Deidre slipped her arm around his waist. "My darling husband, you truly are the shepherd here in Renwick."

He nodded. "A poor one when the flock wishes to run amok, which seems to be happening more frequently, the older I grow."

"Is that really any different from every day?" She knew he blamed himself when his parishioners failed to follow his counsel. "Your duty is to guide with faith, and console with love. The rest you must leave in God's hands, no matter how difficult that is."

Jeffrey kissed her brow. "You always see what I do not."

"And I never wear silly hats," she added with a smile.

A loud thumping on the door of the parsonage made Jeffrey frown, and he hurried with her to find a very pale Margaret Reed hovering on the doorstep, her hand pressed to her heaving bosom, too winded to speak. Mud dripped from her garments and encrusted the too-large boots she wore,

"I will fetch the smelling salts," Deidre told her husband, only to find a restraining hand on her arm.

"Please, I am well." Margaret dragged in some air. "If I might rest for a moment, and catch my breath. I rode here from the Tindall's on horseback."

Jeffrey looked astounded. "By yourself, in the dark?"

They ushered her into the sitting room, where he eased her down on their chaise while Deidre lit the lamps. She debated on whether or not to get the small bottle of brandy they kept for medicinal use, but decided against it when she saw the color returning to the older woman's cheeks.

"Forgive me for intruding at such a late hour," Margaret said, her voice still slightly breathless but steadier. "I could not think of what else to do."

Jeffrey knelt down beside her. "What has happened, Mrs. Reed?"

"It is Jennet." She drew in a deep breath.

"I sent our man Barton to Tindall House to await her return from the masquerade ball. I did not wish her to drive to Reed Park alone, you see, after she left Catherine there. I have seen strange men walking about our grounds at night. Men not of Renwick or any of the estates, and now she has not come home."

"I saw your daughter just before we left the ball," Deidre told her before glancing quickly at her husband. "She looked very well. She must have stayed a little longer to enjoy the dancing."

"That cannot be." Margaret swiped at her eyes. "Barton came back to tell me that Catherine returned without her, and then our carriage vanished entirely. My Jennet is stranded at that horrible house. I cannot ride all the way out there, for I do not know the roads. I will be thrown from the horse for certain."

Deidre had felt uneasy from the moment she and Jeffrey had entered Dredthorne Hall. Something about the old house made her feel as if dark forces gathered there. Now she wondered if Jennet might have eloped with the baron, or if the house had claimed yet another victim.

"I will drive our carriage out there directly myself," Jeffrey said, reaching for his cloak. "You stay here and rest until I come back with your daughter. It will be well, Mrs. Reed, I promise you."

"Thank you, Vicar." Margaret fell back against the cushions. "God bless you for being such a friend to us."

Draping the shivering woman with her shawl, Deidre met her husband's determined gaze. "Be careful, my dear."

Once outside the hidden library, Greystone gestured for Jennet to stop and stay where she was while he went to the door leading out to the hall. There he eased it open to a small gap and peered out.

Three men dressed in great coats and masks carried Arthur Pickering's body past him, heading for the kitchens. Likely they would put his body with Foray's, where it would remain concealed until the smell of rot or the need for firewood brought the servants. He imagined they had already tidied the scene of the murder.

Greystone had never cared for Arthur, or his macabre sense of humor, but he had been a skilled agent and an excellent courier. His loss would be felt on both sides of the channel.

Carefully he closed the door and leaned back against it. He saw how Jennet was staring at him, and the rapidly-darkening bruise on her face. He wanted to stalk out and gut all three of the brutes for daring to strike her, but that would have to wait. Somehow he had to get her out of the house and to safety, and take care of the package.

Then he would deal with the killers.

Greystone took hold of her hand, and led her into the adjoining smoking room, which stood dark, but had a window facing the front drive.

"What are you doing?" she whispered as he tried to open the window.

"Quiet." He waved her back and shifted to one side as he saw a slim figure approaching the steps.

The new arrival wore a heavy hooded cloak that covered body and face, but he could see boots and dark trousers as the folds of the cloak moved. The men who had killed Foray and Pickering would answer to this one, Greystone suspected. Since he knew they had not found what they had killed for, they would next begin searching the house.

Identifying the ringleader might well expose an entire network of French agents working in England.

He waited until the cloaked figure had entered the house before he moved back to Jennet. "Another has come. I must go upstairs. Hide under the dining room table. They will not think to look for you there."

"You expect me to cower away while you dart about with killers in the place?" She shook her head. "On the contrary. I am not leaving your side, sir."

Greystone knew arguing with her was pointless; she had that stubborn gleam in her eye now.

"Take off your gown." When her jaw sagged, he took hold of her skirt and shook it, rustling the old silk. "It makes too much noise when you move. I will give you my shirt to wear."

For a moment it looked as if she might argue the point, and then she turned and presented her back to him. "Unfasten me, please."

Greystone used his dagger to slice through the fastenings, and then played lady's maid as he helped her out of the old blue gown. He tried to avert his gaze while he removed his shirt, but the sight of her in her undergarments proved irresistible. With but a few layers of thin cotton and linen veiling her body, her long, elegant limbs and slight but shapely curves enticed him. The only improvement would be to strip her down to her skin so he could see the lamplight on her.

God, but she was lovely.

Jennet planted her hands on her hips. "This might have been your pleasure every night and morning, my lord, had you kept your promise to me," she whispered fiercely. "Think on that as you ogle."

"That I have." More than he cared to admit to himself, in fact. Had a day passed that he had not thought of her? Greystone could not recall.

As he bared his chest she stared and then sighed. "And now I do the same to you.

We are beyond all propriety, I suppose. Why must you go upstairs? We could climb out the window there, and run for the nearest neighbor's house."

"There may be more men outside on patrol, and I must retrieve what they have come to steal before the others find it. Also, the damned window has been nailed shut." He draped her with his shirt, which hung down to her knees, and felt her shiver. "Do not be afraid."

"You did not ignore your mother's warnings to come here," Jennet muttered. "If I live to see the morrow, I will never hear the end of it."

"You will live," Greystone said as he finished buttoning the placket, and then rested his hands on her shoulders. "Hide beneath the table, please. I will retrieve what I need and come back for you."

"They have already caught you once, and bashed you on the head. If they return and find us gone, they will search and find me." She sniffed. "Besides that, you are a terrible spy. I am not allowing you out of my sight."

"If they catch us, they will try to use you to make me talk," Greystone warned her. "To them we are the enemy, and they would do terrible things to us both, things worse than death."

She paled. "Why?"

"They want something from me, and I cannot permit them to have it." He stroked his hands down her arms. "I will not surrender you or myself to them. Death is kinder than what they intend. Do you understand me?"

"Of course." Jennet swallowed hard and blinked quickly. "I have no desire to… You will be quick about it? So that it does not hurt?"

"If it comes to that, yes." He thumbed a tear from her cheek before he kissed her brow. "Stay at my side now, and move as quietly as you can."

Greystone took her hand in his. They walked out into the dining room, where he waited at the door and listened before stepping out. Sounds coming from the study told him they were searching that room; they likely presumed Pickering had kept the Raven's delivery close to him.

Only when they found nothing would they come back to the hidden library. He returned to the dining room, and went to the back wall to close the Pandora panel. Inserting his pick from the front, he bent and snapped off the tip of it inside the lock.

The broken piece of pick would prevent them from opening the panel with a key; they would assume he and Jennet had jammed it from the other side. Forcing it to get inside would take time and tools. It might be another hour before they discovered their captives had already escaped.

To her credit Jennet moved as surely and silently as Greystone did when he led her out to the stairs. When they reached the second floor he gestured for her to stop while he moved onto the landing. Once he determined no one else occupied the floor, he beckoned to her, and took her into his bed chamber. Once he closed the door Greystone quickly checked the safeguards he had left behind. The undisturbed markers told him no one had yet searched the room.

"In here," he told her, picking up a lamp and walking into the dressing room.

* * *

JENNET HAD no notion of what Greystone had hidden in the small room, and wondered what could be so important that he would risk both their lives to retrieve it. She watched him as he picked up and moved aside the wash stand, and then knelt on the floor. After removing a cut section of floor board, he reached down and drew out a long, scuffed leather case with the most peculiar straps.

"We will have to wait before we try to leave the hall," he told her. "Once they have finished searching the first floor, they will go to the hidden library to question us. That will be our chance."

Her brows rose. "That is why you broke off that tool in the lock, to hamper their entry."

Greystone nodded, and gave her a look of approval. "Such impediments are often the best distractions."

From the case he took out a coil of wire,

some vials filled with clouded liquid, and several palm-size blades that had no hilts. He put back the vials, but tucked the rest of the items into his belt and pockets. He then produced a pair of long-barreled pistols and a small sack, from which he drew a handful of heavy, sharp-studded brass rings.

Jennet had never seen so many weapons or such unattractive jewelry.

"Why would a spy need eight ugly rings?" she demanded in a whisper.

He made a fist and tapped the base of his knotted fingers. "When I wear them and hit someone, they do a great deal of damage."

Appalled now, she drew back. "You said you played a merchant in France. Merchants do not beat people."

"I play a merchant so that I might travel freely." He checked the pistols, but his mouth flattened. "Do not ask me more."

He kept fending off every inquiry she made, as if she were some stranger to him. It was not to be borne.

"I consented to have you kill me if we are caught," Jennet reminded him. "I woke you in the library. Before that, I gave myself to you in the hot house. I have trusted you, far beyond my better judgment, yet you persist in concealing yourself and your actions from me." She folded her arms. "I am asking more, sir."

He set aside the pistols and came to close the door to the bed chamber. "Keep your voice down."

She hadn't realized she was almost shouting at him. As he moved toward his ghastly collection of weapons Jennet took hold of his arm to stop him, and stood on her toes to put her mouth next to his ear.

"This is about you, Liam, not me. Since the day you left I have wondered what, exactly, made you do it," she said in her lowest, sweetest voice. "If nothing more, I have earned the truth. Before either of us flee or die, you will tell me the reason why you left Renwick. Or I will put on your ugly rings and hit you until you do."

Greystone drew back, walked to the other side of the dressing room, and then returned to her. The look on his face was one of exasperated resignation.

"I am not merely a spy." He finally met

her gaze, his own shuttered. "If you must know, then I will tell you. I serve the crown as an assassin. I am known as the Raven."

Jennet had thought she could not ever feel as angry as she had after they had made love, and she had struck him in the face. Alas, she had been wrong. "You left me to do this. To become this…this…Raven. So you could go to France, and spy, and kill people."

"My targets have been dangerous and vicious men who would do their worst to ensure Bonaparte's victory," he assured her. "Interrogators, torturers, and the very worst of brutes from the battlefield. I took no pleasure in it, but for every life I have taken, I have saved thousands."

"That is not the material point here." She took in a deep breath. "You chose to become an assassin instead of my husband. You did not marry me because of this. Have I got that right?"

Greystone nodded once.

Jennet could not hit him again. She could not scream. She had no poison. She might use one of his blades to stab him in his black heart, but that would leave her alone to face Pickering's murderers. She glanced around her, seized the basin from the wash stand, and hurled its contents into his face. He stood there, soaked and dripping, streams of water pouring down his cheeks like tears. She saw some shining rivulets streak his chest, and realized the dousing had removed the silver from his hair.

"Do you feel better now?" he muttered.

"I am trapped in this house with a dead man and his killers. I am wearing the shirt of an assassin to whom I gave myself seven years after he fled on our wedding day. Which he did so he could kill the very worst of the French." Oddly saying it aloud calmed her, and she traced the gleaming marks the dye had left on his skin. "Do you know, I have never felt better in my life."

"KEEP TOUCHING ME," Greystone warned, "and you may revise that opinion."

If nothing else, Jennet had settled their accounts and satisfied her pride. Now it cost her nothing to slide her hands up the slick, muscular vault of his chest, and link her fingers behind his neck. The movement brought her body against his, and the warmth of him came through the borrowed shirt and spread over her breasts. She could feel his arms coming around her, the new tautness in his limbs, the swelling bulge of his shaft against her belly.

"I am willing to have my mind changed," Jennet told him.

"There is no time for this," he said against her hair as he clamped his hands around her waist, as if he meant to push her away. "I know you must despise me for the work I do."

"You said yourself that we must wait until those men enter the library." She pressed herself against him. "And I do not despise you. Before he died, my father did the same," she said, startling him. "I cannot tell you how many men he killed while fighting for England, but I wager there were many. My mother told me that he was an expert marksman with any weapon, and he even taught her how to be a crack shot. Why did you keep all this from me?"

"I never wished you to know the truth."

He drew back, his eyes filled with torment. "I wanted you to see me as the man you loved."

"Except for this hair dye, you do look remarkably similar to him." She pressed her lips to his jaw. "Perhaps I should examine more of you to be sure."

Greystone uttered a muffled groan. "Jenny, please."

"Or I could simply kiss you breathless and then ravish you, as you did to me in the gardens and the hot house," Jennet suggested, nudging him back to the bench by the wash stand. "Well, I could not carry you off–"

He covered her mouth with his, stroking her lips apart with his tongue to give her a deep, hungry kiss as she pushed him down to sit on the cushion. Straddling his lap felt as natural as reaching down to release his straining manhood from his trousers. His hands took hold of her waist again, lifting her as he guided his cock between her thighs. When she felt him nudge her quim, she sank down slowly, taking him inside her.

"Ah." Tucking her knees on either side

of his hips, and bracing herself with her hands on his shoulders, Jennet engulfed his thick girth. She glanced down as his hands unfastened the shirt and unlaced her soft stays until he freed her aching breasts. "You have no respect for my modesty, sir."

"My cock is so deep inside you, Jenny, I can feel you melting around me like hot honey," Greystone said softly as he put his hands on her mounds, and slowly rubbed them. "I believe I have obliterated your modesty."

"Good." She smiled at him. "It has been growing tiresome."

His touch felt so wonderful she could hardly breathe, and then he brought his mouth to her, and began kissing and licking and sucking at her. Jennet lifted herself from him, and then came down, stroking him with her softness as he ravished her nipples. One of his long, lovely hands stroked down her spine, and then cupped and squeezed the curve of her bottom, making her gasp with excitement.

"You should not be touching that, you wicked man, nor kissing my breasts," she pretended to scold him. "It is simply not done."

"Had we time enough, I would take you out to that bed and strip you naked," Greystone said, his voice deep and rough now. "I would map every inch of you with my hands. And my mouth. And my cock."

"You intrigue me now." From some hints in novels she had read, Jennet had long suspected there could be other ways to make love. "You wish to kiss other parts of me, perhaps?"

"I have dreamed of it," he assured her, and rubbed his thumb across her lips. "And imagined you doing the same to me. So many dark nights I have lain alone in my bed, stroking my cock with my hand, and wondering if you would dare do so with your mouth. How it would look, to behold you suckling me."

"That is very shocking, my lord." She pouted for a moment, and then smiled. "I think I should like to try, but only if you will do the same to me."

"I knew it would be like this with you," Greystone muttered, almost as if he were angry. "I could see the passion waiting to awaken in you. I could feel it every time I touched you."

She looked into his eyes. "Then why did you leave me to go and kill people, you idiot?"

A loud crash came from the floor below, and they both went still. Jennet held her breath as she listened for the sound of footsteps on the stairs, but none came.

"I fear we must be quick now," she murmured against his ear.

"Hold onto me." He stood, pressing her to him so that their bodies remained joined, and then lowered her onto her back on the bench.

Jennet wrapped her legs around his hips as he began to thrust into her, his shaft driving deep and hard into her clenching slickness. Greystone never looked away from her face, and when he saw her press her lips together he clamped a hand over her mouth to help her silence her cries. She writhed under him, helpless now as a rush of sensations tossed her higher and higher with each plunge of his hips. He felt her teeth against his palm and gripped her breast with his other hand, tugging at her nipple until she arched up and then shook as her terrible need became an incandescent ecstasy.

Greystone muttered something dark and desirous as he plowed through her pleasure and found his own. He thrust one last time, his cock pumping again and again as he filled her with his seed. He braced an arm over her as he held her skewered, her mouth panting and her skin flushed rosy, and kissed her with the delicate tenderness of a hopeful swain before disengaging their bodies. He sat on the floor by the bench, his head resting against her hip.

"You have undone me, Liam." Jennet brushed the damp hair back from his face.

He caught her hand, and kissed her palm. "That night at the harvest dance, when you stood by the window to eavesdrop," he said as he laced his fingers through hers. "Do you remember it?"

"I can hardly forget." She wished she could go back to that night. She would have eloped with him on the spot. "Why do you think on it?"

"I saw you there before I came out of the hall. The quiet child I had met in church had grown into the most striking woman I had ever seen." He turned to regard her, his eyes filled with emotion. "I can still see you, grown tall and shapely. Your body seemed as refined and elegant as if you had been sculpted from sunlit marble. You wore no jewelry or hair adornments, only a bronze velvet ribbon around your neck."

"Catherine said it would disguise my goose neck." She smiled, remembering. "She always wore them in those days, before they became unfashionable."

"You might have dressed as the other ladies had, in a pastel dress with a satin sash. Instead you wore dark green velvet, like some goddess of the garden." Greystone shifted so he loomed over her, and cradled her face between his hands. "I looked into your eyes, as pure and new as ever the world is at spring, and I lost all sense of myself. From that night on there could be no more loneliness for me. My world became us, together. Always."

Jennet felt confused by the intensity of his words. Was he trying to apologize again for leaving her? She would not revisit that subject, not now.

"We must live through this night so we can be as you envisioned us," she told him.

The pleasure emptied out of his eyes. "We can never be that."

"We were just now." Jennet pushed herself upright. "Surely you can give up this life as an assassin. It is not who you are."

"The quickest way to get out of the hall unseen is by the staircase tower," Greystone told her as he rose and went to the clothespress and removed a shirt. He quickly donned it and went back to his cache of weapons. "Go down the hall to the very end, turn right, and then left through the door to the stairs."

"What are you talking about?" she demanded as she fastened her soft stays and his shirt.

"Your escape. I will lure them from the house while you escape." He handed her a dagger and a small pistol, pressing them into her hands when she wouldn't take them. "When you reach the bottom of the stairs, walk straight ahead. The door there leads to the outside."

Jennet shook her head. "You must come with me. Liam."

"I must do my work now, and you cannot be part of that," he told her. "Stay out of sight as you make your way to the road; they may have men out patrolling the grounds." He gave her a hard, brief kiss and then strode out.

Ruban upended the desk where Pickering had died, sending the drawers and their contents flying. Kicking a boot through the scattered papers did not provide any consolation. Whatever the English agent had stolen from the officer's tent back in France remained hidden somewhere inside the house, or concealed on the Raven himself.

Staring at the puddle of blood Pickering had left behind made Ruban even more furious. He should have died after being questioned, not before. If he had been the Raven, then finding whatever he had spirited back to England would be almost impossible.

Ruban knelt and began sifting through

the detritus, most of which dated back a century. Beneath a pile of receipts lay a small black notebook stamped in gold with Pickering's initials. Opening it revealed pages of spidery writing, all in English, that detailed times, dates and remote locations across England. A single word had been noted at the end of each entry: Dispatches. Ledger. Weapons. Informant.

Already familiar with such records, Ruban now knew that Arthur Pickering had been an important courier for the English war effort. He would be sent to retrieve acquisitions too sensitive or dangerous to risk transporting openly. Bonaparte had a network of the same that he used to send and receive messages across France.

"He was not the Raven." Ruban felt relieved and dismayed, for that meant the assassin was still at large.

The last entry in the notebook corresponded with the time, date and location of Pickering's masquerade tonight. Beneath it he had written a single, damning word.

Cipher.

Now the reason the traitor at the chateau had killed himself became only too clear. The man had somehow stolen the cipher used by the Emperor's officers, and passed it on to the Raven. All troop movements, battle plans, and every other effort vital to the French war effort were written in code that could only be decrypted by one cipher. The Raven would have to bring it to England, where it could be distributed by Wellington to all of his officers in the field. Once they had it, they would be able to read any communique they captured, or use it to send false messages to their enemy.

To prevent that, the only solution would be to change the cipher, Ruban thought. Yet with the French forces fighting in so many locations at present that would take weeks. In the meantime, the English could cause irreparable harm; perhaps even turn the tide of the war against Bonaparte.

If Pickering had not been the Raven, then he had come here to meet the assassin and take possession of the cipher. Which meant another man at the ball had come for that purpose. He would be someone who did not live in the village, but only came to visit infrequently, perhaps for the first time in many years.

Ruban realized who that was, and swore.

CHAPTER 18

He had given her the weapons, Jennet thought as she made her way out to the hall, where she stood listening before she approached the stairs. He had only himself to blame if she shot him—which she would, if she found him before the French agents did.

Am I a simpleton, that I keep repeating the same mistake over and over?

She tucked the dagger in the lacings of her stays—she had no other place to put it —but kept the pistol in her hand as she took the stairs one at a time. She could hear voices now coming from the kitchens, angry voices arguing in French. One belonged to the brute who had ordered the men to put her in the library, but the other sounded strangely high-pitched and shrill, like that of a child having a tantrum.

Jennet peeked into the dining room to make sure it was empty before she approached the closed door to the kitchens.

"Why did you kill Pickering?" the childish voice demanded in French. "Your orders were to keep him alive, you piece of shit."

Not a child, but a woman, Jennet realized. From the ease with which she cursed she must be a Frenchwoman. But if that were the case, why did her voice make all the hair on Jennet's nape stand on end?

"He put de documents into de fire," the brute said sullenly. "Jacques tried to stop him."

"Those documents are the deeds to the house, imbecile," the woman snapped. "He was the courier, which is why he wanted you to kill him before I arrived. He knew too much to risk being interrogated. That is how fucking clever he was. Where is Greystone?"

"We lock him and de girl in de cache room," the man said.

"At least you did that much right." The

woman said something else in a lower voice.

"Here?" the brute asked, as if surprised.

"Here." Dishes clattered as if dropping to the floor. "I need it. Give it to me, now."

Realizing they might come out to try and access the hidden library, Jennet hurried back out into the hall. More voices drew near from the opposite direction, and she looked around quickly before she stepped into a coat closet and pulled the door almost shut. Through the crack she watched as the three masked agents came from the reception room and went toward the kitchens. In another moment they would come out and discover the jammed lock. Did she remain hidden, or try to run? She still didn't know where Greystone was.

Then she saw him, walking straight for the dining room, and wondered if now she would even get a chance to kill him before the French did.

Now who is the child having a tantrum? Her sensibility drawled. *You have fallen in love again with the scoundrel. Do something before he walks into that nest of vipers.*

As soon as Greystone came within reach

of the coat closet Jennet opened the door, seized his arm and dragged him inside with her. He clamped his hand around her throat so severely she could not breathe or move, but just as suddenly he released her, and eased the door shut. Then he pulled her into his arms, and held her for the space of a breath before drawing back.

"I told you to get out of the house," he muttered, cradling her face between his hands. "You were supposed to escape this madness."

"The villains are in the kitchens," she whispered back. "I heard them quarreling. One is a woman, and she seems to have charge of the others. She used very coarse language while admonishing them for killing Mr. Pickering. I do not know what they are doing now, but it involves breaking dishes."

"A woman." He sounded as if she had punched him in the face again. "No, you must be mistaken. Ruban is a Frenchman."

"It does not matter who or what this Ruban is. I will not leave you here to be murdered like Mr. Pickering." She thought for a moment. "There are two of us, and at least four of them. We must employ a ruse to reduce their numbers. I will go back upstairs and scream, and that should draw out at least two of them. Then you can surprise the others—"

Greystone put his mouth over hers, muffling the rest of what she meant to say. He kissed her with singular absorption, not as he had in the garden or the bed chamber, but in the manner she imagined he would before the altar, when they married.

He broke off the kiss to tuck her face against his shoulder, his hand stroking her neck. "You are the most stubborn woman alive," he said as he pressed his cheek to her hair. "I wish to keep you that way."

"Then allow me to be your partner now," Jennet said. "We have to do something before they find us."

"I love you." He pressed a kiss to her head. "I have since the second time I saw you. I wish I could say the first, but that would be unseemly as well as untrue. I tried to forget you, but I could not. I carried you with me everywhere I went."

"You are being ridiculous." She held onto him as a slight dizziness came over her. "We can talk about the past later. The time to act is now."

"I must give you something for sakekeeping." Greystone pressed his thumb under her jaw. "It is the reason they killed Pickering. Give it to the magistrate, and tell him it is to be taken to London, and delivered to the Secretary at War. It must be placed in his hands directly. You must not fail in this. Tell me that you do not hate me."

"I love you." Jennet felt his thumb pressing harder now, and realized what he meant to do. As her head spun wildly she tried to push him away. "No, Liam. Please."

"Forgive me, Jenny," Greystone said as he pinned her against the side of the closet.

* * *

WHEN JENNET WENT limp Greystone caught her and lowered her to the floor of the closet. Although he knew he had used only enough pressure to render her unconscious, he kept his hand on her neck. Feeling the throb of her pulse remain steady strengthened his resolve. He covered all but her face with coats and then turned her head away from the door before he stepped out.

The sounds drifting from the kitchens no longer sounded like voices; instead he heard a soft keening mixed with low, harsh grunts. Drawing his daggers, he approached the entry to the dining room and stood to one side to scan the room, which appeared empty. The door to the kitchens stood partly open, and through it he could see one of the brutes pinning a small, writhing form down on a work table as he hunched and jerked—and what he was doing was unmistakable.

Greystone felt sickened as he crossed the room, changing the angle of his advance so that he stayed out of the Frenchman's sight. Only when he saw the child had Catherine Tindall's face did he forget all of his training to rush through the door and jerk the brute away from her.

"Run," he told Jennet's friend as he turned on the agent, his daggers ready. "You think you can treat a lady like a whore, you animal?"

The Frenchman smirked. "Ah, but mon ami, she is my whore."

Something grabbed Greystone's leg from behind and pulled it out from under him, sending him sprawling. As he flipped over, Catherine planted her boot on his neck, and pointed a small pistol at his face.

"Hello, William," she said, using one hand to tug up and fasten the man's breeches she wore. "Rather rude of you to interrupt us, but I suppose it looked rather bad. Jean-Pierre likes it rough, you see. Then again, so do I."

Greystone blinked. "Catherine?"

"Call me what the French do," she chided. "Ruban."

Everything came clear to him in a rush: how Ruban had been able to hide for so long on English soil, the remarkable amount of intelligence he gathered, and why he never allowed anyone who had seen his face to live.

No one could know that the sadistic brute who inspired terror in some many was a petite, delicate-looking woman.

As he surged up Catherine rammed her boot against his throat and cocked the gun. "Put down the blades, my lord, or I will shoot you now." She shifted the angle of her aim to his lower abdomen. "Men can live without their cock and ballocks. I have parted several from their treasures. You will not wish to live once I have, of course, but that is not my concern."

Greystone released the hilts, and the daggers clattered to the floor beside him. "How is it that you are Ruban?" He still couldn't quite believe it.

"The Minister of Police named me that, for the ribbons I wore around my neck. A little reminder of all those who met Monsieur Guillotine during the revolution." Catherine wrinkled her nose. "Rather passé now." To Jean-Pierre she said, "Mon couer, do get that coil of rope we brought, and a nice, sturdy chair for the gentleman." She returned her attention to Greystone. "What have you done with Jennet Reed, William? Before you lie, I know my men put you both in the hidden library."

"She's gone. I told her to run while you were searching the study." He prayed she remained unconscious long enough to save her life. "How did you come to serve Bonaparte? You are as English as I am."

"I would set fire to myself if I was," she

assured him. "Long before my family became the Tindalls, they were the Tullys."

Greystone blinked. "You are Irish."

"Aye, and the prettiest of my line." Her voice took on a distinctly different accent. "From the shadows we Tullys have been fighting for Erin for generations. My grandparents created the Tindalls, so we might pose as part of English society. But our efforts cost a great deal, you see."

Any hope to persuade her with an offer of a pardon if she came over to his side died in that moment. Even he had heard whispers of the Tullys, said to be the most pitiless and secretive of the northern rebels. He also knew her kind despised his government so much they would rather die than accept amnesty.

It also made sense of why she would serve the enemy. "The French pay their spies very well."

"More than you can imagine. My family went in with them for the coin," Catherine said, using her upper-class English voice as if to mock him. "For me, the lure was always the work. I discovered during my training that I have a true talent for it." She shrugged. "And the fucking. I do enjoy that as well."

Jean-Pierre returned with the chair and the rope, and hauled him from the floor before he tied him up. Catherine stepped back and kept the pistol leveled at his head the entire time, so Greystone didn't try to resist. Once he had been secured, she tucked the pistol away and began rummaging through the cabinets.

"I will question him," she told Jean-Pierre in French as she began assembling a collection of kitchen knives. "Go and collect the others, and prepare the horses. Then search the rooms upstairs. If you see the girl, do not harm her. Bring her to me."

"Jacques wants a taste of her," Jean-Pierre said in the same language, and gave Greystone a broad smile. "Maybe you let him do her on the kitchen table after you kill this one, eh? You know how you like to watch them cry and beg."

Catherine turned around and regarded him.

Her lover lifted his hands. "I want you to be happy, that is all."

"I will be happy when we are back in

Paris." She picked up a carving knife and used it to point to the door. "Go."

Ignoring their gruesome hilarity required all of Greystone's concentration, for he had very little time left to decide how to manage the situation. He had never been captured, and all of his vials of poison remained concealed upstairs. This was what Pickering had faced at his end, and he had goaded the agents into killing him.

Somehow he must do the same.

"I am sorry about that," Catherine said as she came over to him with a carving knife. "You know how trying it can be, working with Jean-Pierre's sort. All ballocks and no brains. But now we must move on to the interrogation. Where have you hidden Jennet Reed?"

"As I told you, she left. I told her where to find my horse, and what to do as soon as she got home." Greystone stared past her. "Likely she has arrived at Reed Park by now, and is sending her man for the magistrate."

"Well, if that is true, we will make that our next stop." She expertly sliced open the front of his shirt. "A pity, too, for I had hoped to preserve my friendship with your lady love. Her goodness often grows monotonous, but she has provided excellent cover whenever I must decamp to the country."

"Leave her out of this," he said tonelessly. "She is a civilian."

"That is the problem with you English. You regard women as beneath you, unable to be your partners in the war effort. In Erin, we are all soldiers." She began ripping off his shirt with the efficiency of someone who had done the same many times.

"Jennet is an innocent," Greystone reminded her.

Catherine chuckled. "That she is. I am sure it will be vastly entertaining to reveal my true self to her before I cut her throat. Never would she have suspected her giddy friend to be an agent for the French. Her talent for reading people never worked on me."

"She loves you as a friend." It would break her heart when she discovered Catherine's deception, too. "We never expect the people we care for to be heartless monsters, and that is your specialty, isn't it? Your life is nothing but one endless masquerade."

"You say that with such disapproval." She made a tsking sound. "I know you are the Raven, William. You can stop pretending you care for anything but the next kill."

"Jennet need never know the truth about either of us," Greystone said quickly. "You have shown yourself only to me. I will die here tonight, and she will believe I have abandoned her again. You can still be her friend."

"True, if I wished to." She tossed the torn garment aside and stood back as if admiring his bare chest. "I am not entirely heartless, William. Before my men killed Pickering, I pleasured him twice—once with my mouth. While I was searching his bed chamber he came in, you see, so I was obliged to play the swooning maid for his benefit."

"Arthur was only a courier," Greystone told her.

"So, it seems. Still, I can assure you that he died a happy man." She ran her finger down his sternum and stroked his abdomen. "Would you care for one last romp, my lord? I've always wondered what sort of lover you would prove. Jean-Pierre told me you were quite vigorous with Jennet in the hot-house."

Her touch felt cold, and her fingers hard as bone, as if a skeleton caressed him. "I cannot *not* oblige you, madam."

Catherine grabbed his crotch, but when she felt no sign of arousal from him she lifted her hand and slapped his face. She strode away from him, her fists clenched, her back rigid. Just as suddenly she turned around, her expression serene.

"A pity, for now I must seek my amusements elsewhere," Catherine said in a pleasant tone. "I know just the thing I will do. When we arrive at Reed Park, I will permit Jacques and Jean-Pierre to have Margaret while I force Jennet to watch. Do you think the old lady can accommodate them both at once? Or perhaps I will take both ladies with me to Paris, and allow them to entertain some of my friends there."

"You will not touch them," Greystone said, snarling the words.

"Their fate depends entirely on how cooperative you are, William." She came over and stroked his face where she had marked it. "What will it be: a quick death for your lady love and her sniveling mother, or a command performance with my men, or months of servicing the Emperor's worst? The last is not a reprieve, I assure you. Those fellows in our prisons are much rougher than Jean-Pierre, I fear. Your contact's mistress held out only a few days before she confessed all, and she had been as well-used as an alley slut before I gave her to them. She was happy to die."

Catherine would take pleasure in keeping her horrific promises; in her role as Ruban she had done far worse. "What do you want to know?"

"I already know that you came here to deliver the cipher to Pickering," she said as she brought her blade to his chest. "Tell me where you have hidden it."

CHAPTER 19

The moon shone down on Jeffrey Branwen like a baleful eye as he slowed the carriage to a stop beside the twin lions guarding the gate to Dredthorne Hall. Peering at the front of the house, he saw most of the windows had gone dark. No carriages occupied the drive, and the carts used by the staff Pickering had hired for the party had also gone. It seemed the ball was over, and all was as it should be.

The memory of seeing Jennet Reed in William Gerard's arms came back to Jeffrey, as if to shame him.

Perhaps she had chosen to stay the night with her former betrothed. A sinful decision, but he knew her attachment to William had never truly been broken. Love such as hers often led to reckless behavior. Yet Jennet had always been a devoted daughter who had attended to her fretful, excitable mother without complaint. He knew she took it upon herself to soothe Margaret each time she had one of her panicking turns. To purposely distress her mother by spending the night away from Reed Park seemed completely out of character.

She is here, and in some trouble. I know it. I can feel it.

The sound of horse hooves drew Jeffrey's gaze to the side of the house, where three men leading horses appeared. The trio came to tether their mounts near the front entry, which made no sense to him. No gentleman rode at night, even with a full moon overhead. One of the men stepped back and staggered as if he had tripped over a stone, and the other two snickered at him.

"Brûle en l'enfer, salauds," the one who had tripped shouted at them.

As a student at theological college Jeffrey had been required to study French. While he had never learned to speak the language with anything more than mediocre fluency, he understood enough to translate the curse.

Burn in hell, you bastards.

Being the vicar of Renwick for nearly twenty years gave him an intimate knowledge of his parish as well. None of the families or their servants spoke French as this man had. The few travelers who came through the area did speak to each other in their own language mixed with some Welsh, but it bore no resemblance to French.

These men did not belong here, not while England engaged in a war with France.

Climbing down from the driver's perch, Jeffrey released the skidpan to keep the horses from wandering off with the carriage. He then watched from the gate as the three men entered the house. They swaggered, as if confident, and servants never came into a great house through the front entry.

Something was indeed very wrong here, and Jennet must have gotten caught up in it.

Jeffrey would never admit it to his wife,

but he secretly disliked Dredthorne Hall as much as she did. A madman had shot his sister and her future husband in the front hall, leaving them to bleed to death. Some days later Jeffrey had been obliged to leave Lucetta in Deidre's care to hold the funeral services for the assailant and his accomplices. The house had killed them, his wife had once claimed, because it could not have his sister and her beloved. Although as a vicar he could not hold with such superstition, a part of him knew Deidre was right.

Now the French had invaded Dredthorne, it seemed. But what would they want with Arthur Pickering and Jennet Reed?

Jeffrey began walking up the drive, and his dread seemed to swell with every step he took. He was a man of God, not the law. Dealing with the enemy would be better managed by soldiers. Renwick had a magistrate, but his estate bordered the river, and he would likely have retired by this hour. The nearest regiment had been recently moved to Brighton to prepare for their voyage to Spain, to relieve the exhausted English troops there fighting in the Peninsular War.

A passage from Joshua came to him, one he had often paraphrased for his parishioners during their worst moments: Do not be frightened, and do not be dismayed, for He is with you wherever you go.

Jeffrey stopped short of the steps at the front of the house and regarded the horses the men had left there. None of them had come from the livery stable in the village; he had often visited the stable master and knew every horse available for hire there. These animals looked as if they hadn't been groomed or properly looked after for some time.

The brightness of the moonlight allowed him to follow their tracks from the house to the staircase tower. There, where he expected to see them disappear into the stables, they instead led into the trees, as if the men had kept them in the woods behind the hall. If the three men were agents who had come to England for nefarious purposes, the forest would have provided them with concealment for as long as they needed it.

Arthur Pickering did not come to Renwick to hold a masquerade.

Jeffrey took a step toward the staircase tower, and then nearly slipped and fell. He righted himself, and saw something wet on the ground. It had run from the woodpile bin to collect in a small puddle. Too dark and thick to be water, he bent down and smelled a coppery odor coming from it.

Blood.

"Sovereign God, abide with me now." Murmuring that entreaty gave Jeffrey renewed strength, and he approached the bin. Blood stained the ground before disappearing under it, and when he lifted the lid he saw why.

He did not recognize the murdered man, but the quality garments he wore suggested that he worked inside the house, probably as a valet or steward. He had died suddenly and violently, yet someone had put his body here, and closed his eyes. Those two acts implied cunning and sympathy, and a murderer would not feel both at once. He must not have been the first to find the corpse.

Furious indignation rose inside him, making it impossible to pray for the poor man's soul. More than any other sin, murder offended and disgusted Jeffrey. Carefully he closed the lid, resting his hand upon it as he made a silent promise to return as soon as he could, to attend to him properly.

Now he had to find Jennet Reed, before whoever had killed this man did.

CHAPTER 20

Finding her way out of darkness seemed impossible, so Jennet went to another, happier place in her dreams.

In the beginning she had not been very happy about that particular evening. Time and again she had tried to talk her mother out of attending Lady Hardiwick's spring dance, but Margaret would not hear of it. Spending a month in bed with a nasty head cold had left her mother pale and exhausted, and genuinely in need of rest. Yet Margaret strangely determined to go out into society.

"We cannot stay shut up in this house another evening," her mother declared as she came down stairs from her chamber, her hand clinging tightly to the railing. "I accepted the invitation, so we must make an appearance, or risk offending dear Lady Hardiwick."

"Your voice is shaking," Jennet pointed out as she climbed up the steps to meet her. "So are your knees. I will risk her disapproval."

Margaret glared at her. "You cannot see my knees."

"I can hear them knocking together." She guided her downstairs, where she had hoped to steer her into the sitting room so she could persuade her to instead sit by the fire. When Margaret stopped in the front hall and called for their housekeeper, she knew she would have to try something else. "Please, Mama, you are not well enough to go out. The sickness might return, or even worsen. Surely you do not wish to stay in bed until summer."

"Do not fuss, Jennet." Margaret smiled as their housekeeper appeared. "Ah, Mrs. Holloway. Has Barton brought up the carriage as I instructed?"

The housekeeper's gaze went from

Margaret to Jennet and back again. "Yes, madam."

She smiled her approval. "Then all I need is my wrap and Miss Jennet's jacket, and you have them both. You are a treasure indeed." She turned so the other woman could drape her with the heavy silk and velvet shawl. "Come, now, my darling girl."

Jennet and the housekeeper watched Margaret walk through the front door, her stride as eager as if she meant to go on foot to the Hardiwick's estate.

"She has not been at the wine, I hope," Jennet murmured.

Mrs. Holloway shook her head as she helped her into her jacket. "Nor the laudanum, Miss. I checked the pantry and the medicine cabinet."

Once Barton delivered them to the Hardiwicks' enormous country house, Jennet noticed her mother's step grew slightly less purposeful. By the time they made their way inside and through the receiving line and into the ballroom, Margaret took a turn away from the dance floor. She headed directly for the row of chairs and settees placed against the side wall for the older attendees.

"No one will wish to partner an old lady like me." Her mother craned her neck as if looking for someone, and then grimaced and pressed a hand to the small of her back. "Goodness, I can feel my bones creaking from all those weeks in bed. I must speak to Dr. Mallory about that."

"Really, Mama, we should go home," Jennet said as she guided her over to the most comfortable-looking settee. "You are not up to this yet."

"Nonsense. I am feeling most invigorated." Trembling now, Margaret lowered herself onto the cushions and sighed. "There, that is very good. I am quite cozy now. Is your friend Catherine here?"

Jennet sank down beside her. "She is back in London, I believe." She removed her jacket and draped it over the top of her mother's shawl. "What is this about, Mama, really? I cannot remember the last time you wished to attend a ball. If ever you have."

Margaret absently patted her hand. "I wish to be here with you, and show our dear neighbor how much I appreciate her kind invitation."

"You do not care for Lady Hardiwick," she reminded her. "You think she is a terrible gossip, and an unrepentant snob."

"Just so, my dear," her mother said absently. She seemed fascinated with the lines of dancers weaving in and out of the quadrille, and began tapping the toes of her slippers to the lively Scottish medley being played by the musicians. "They will be playing a reel next. Go and find yourself a partner, my dear, that I may see you dance."

"Every gentleman of my acquaintance is presently engaged, Mama." Jennet made a show of looking around the ballroom. "I cannot present myself to a stranger, nor dance a reel by myself. Besides, I do not wish to leave you alone when you are like this."

"You are becoming a wall flower," her mother scolded, and then her expression softened. "Or I have made you one with all my ailments and sickness. How you must resent the burden I have become of late, and yet you never complain."

"Mama." Jennet took hold of her hand.

"Is that your reason for insisting we attend? For I would much rather stay at home with you."

"That is because you are the very best of daughters, and I the worst of mothers." Margaret touched her handkerchief to her lower eyelids before she shifted to peer through the dancers. "Well, I am old, and very prone to illness, it seems. I should die soon."

"Mama."

"There." Sitting up, her mother pointed her fan at the doorway. "The Gerards have arrived. They have been in the city all of the winter, I should think." She glanced at her for a long moment before she fluttered her fingers beside her temple. "Oh, what is their son's name? I cannot remember."

Jennet glanced at the stern face of Baron Greystone, and the softer, kinder features of his wife. As the Gerards lived most of the year in London they but rarely attended social gatherings in Renwick, so their arrival drew notice from every corner of the room. She did not see their son, but he had probably gone to the card room.

"William," she murmured. "His name is William."

"Yes, of course." Margaret waved to the baroness to catch her attention. "A very kind young gentleman, I am sure. Mrs. Holloway told me that he called five times during my illness, and brought the most beautiful berries from the baroness, do you remember? Oh, do help me up, dear, she is coming."

Jennet braced her mother as she rose, and kept one arm under hers as they both curtseyed to Baroness Greystone, who did the same.

"Margaret, I am so glad to see you recovered." The regal lady smiled at Jennet before she said, "I hope the basket of fruit I sent from the lodge helped in some small way to cheer you."

"Thank you, yes, Amelia." Margaret beamed. "You do grow the sweetest berries in all of the shire, and your note was so welcome."

Jennet felt suspicious now, for she could not recall either woman ever addressing each other with such affectionate informality. "What note was that, Mama?"

Her mother ignored her. "Have you time to sit with me, dear lady? I would love to hear the latest news from London."

"Of course, for I have much to tell you." The baroness immediately sat down in Jennet's spot. "Do go and dance, Miss Reed. I will keep your dear mother company."

Jennet frowned. Her mother had always disliked the city and the society there; she often referred to it as a den of iniquity. Nor had she ever known Lady Greystone to confide anything to Margaret. Yet the two of them had left her no choice but to nod her agreement.

She made her way around the dance floor, but once she was out of her mother's sight she slipped out onto the terrace. A cool breeze greeted her, making her skirts flutter. All of the tension drained out of her as she went to the stone railing bordering the oval veranda. She would stay out here long enough to give the older women time to gossip, and then go in and lie to her mother. She would say she had a dreadful headache and needed to go home. Then she would spend the rest of the night tossing and turning in her bed until she gave herself one, but at least she would be removed from temptation.

"You will find no partners out here, Miss Reed," an amused voice said. "Unless I prove acceptable to you."

"I am not inclined to dance tonight, sir." She didn't look at the man who came to stand beside her. She had instructed the housekeeper to turn him away from Reed Park, which she had five times, but it seemed he meant to persist in his pursuit. "You should see if Miss Hardiwick has yet promised all of hers. She is an enthusiastic dancer, I believe."

"Prudence giggles too much. Also, I think her mother wishes to abduct me and lock me in her daughter's room for a night. I dare not provide her with any such opportunity." A strong hand took hold of hers, clasping it with easy intimacy. "Come and walk with me."

"No." Sometimes the best refusal was the simplest.

"What do you imagine I mean to do, Jenny?" William Gerard tugged her to face him, and his voice dropped low as he added, "Drag you off into the woods there and have my way with you?"

Her heart aquiver now, Jennet placed a restraining hand on his chest. "The last time we were alone together, Liam, you very nearly did."

This secret dance of theirs had been going on since Christmas, when William had caught her under a kissing bough at the village hall. No one had seen him pull her into his arms and covered her mouth with his, but the effect on both of them had been shocking. He had dragged her into another room, where his second kiss turned into an embrace so passionate they had all but undressed each other. He had even tried to convince her to come back to the lodge with him.

He was remembering that night, too; she could see the heat flaring in his wicked green eyes.

"This is how we started the last time we were alone together," Jennet told him, hoping that would cool his ardor. "We must be sensible and avoid making another mistake."

"A mistake?" He sounded distracted, and

had his gaze fixed on her lips. "I would call it a revelation. A glorious, tempestuous miracle that ended far too soon. I swear you have grown more beautiful. How is that possible? When last I saw you, you were perfection."

"Liam, please." She nudged his chin until he looked into her eyes. "I am very flattered, but this is a calamity in the making. Your family doubtless has expectations of you. You will be a baron someday."

"I cannot escape my father's title," he agreed, and cupped her cheek with his hand. "That has nothing to do with us."

"There is no us." And it tore at her heart, but she had to be practical now. "We cannot give in to temptation again. The consequences for us both would be disastrous."

His brows drew together. "I disagree."

"In time you will forget this, ah, infatuation with me," Jennet assured him, "and make a sensible match."

William nodded. "Will you permit me to say—"

"Catherine knows many fine young ladies in the city," she said, smiling as if her heart was not shattering. "Perhaps I might persuade her to–"

"Do shut up, my darling." William pressed a finger to her lips. "I have spoken to my mother about her expectations, and settled them. Tomorrow she and I will talk with my father, and then we will all come to Reed Park to sit down with your mother."

"Why would you…" Her eyes widened as he went down on one knee. "Oh, no. You cannot be serious."

"You will not dance with me. I cannot take you into the woods and ravish you. I can think of nothing else—the ravishing, I fear, not the dancing—yet you will not abandon your inflexible morals. We are at an impasse." He looked up at her, his eyes shining. "Then there is the fact that somehow we have fallen madly in love with each other."

"You noticed," she said faintly.

"Our mothers have, which means everyone has. Only one solution, really." He brought her hand to his lips. "Miss Reed, would you do me the honor of becoming my wife?"

Jennet pressed her palm to his cheek,

savoring the moment before she answered him. "Yes, Mr. Gerard. I will marry you."

I WILL MARRY YOU.

Opening her eyes to darkness, Jennet pushed at the mound of coats covering her until she freed her arms. Her hand went to her throat, which felt tender but not bruised. If Liam had meant to kill her, she would be dead. Instead he had done something to make her swoon so he could leave her here, and then piled coats atop her to conceal her.

That wretched, pig-headed, insidiously noble dolt of a man.

Something with an odd shape shifted in her bodice as she sat up, and she reached in to extract what felt like a thin, narrow, tightly-bound book.

I must give you something for safe-keeping. It is the reason they killed Pickering.

Terror rose inside her in a cold, icy rush. Liam would not have asked her to keep it safe unless he knew that he could not. Even with his skills, she thought it unlikely he could defeat three agents by himself. He intended to sacrifice himself to protect her and the book, and had knocked her out to assure she could not interfere.

He means to leave me again—permanently.

Jennet groped until she found a coat with a loose lining, and tore it partly away from the collar seam. She then worked the book into the tear, and shook the garment until she felt it drop down to the hem. She pushed her arms into the sleeves as she donned the coat, and plucked out her hair pins. Once she had spread her thick tresses over her shoulders and back to conceal the tear, she stood and put her ear against the door.

She could hear the muffled sound of two voices, one of which she knew to be Liam's. They were speaking in French.

A strange sense came over Jennet as she took hold of the door knob. She felt her skin cool, and her muddled thoughts clear. She also no longer felt alone, as if others had slipped into the closet unseen and now stood around her in the darkness.

Emerson Thorne had warned her of

this: *Tonight, every soul lost within these rooms has been awakened. Most intend only to wander, but among them walk malevolent and vengeful spirits that one should not cross.*

The legend of Dredthorne Hall had it that many of its mistresses had died within its walls. If she and Liam were doomed to share their fate, so be it, Jennet thought. She would not surrender to the curse, however, without fighting for her love and their lives.

Yet if she won that battle, perhaps it would break the curse once and for all.

"Please help me save him," she whispered, and thought she felt the coolness around her increase. Her eyes widened as the door to the closet slowly creaked open, showing her the empty hall outside. Never again would she claim not to believe in spirits. "Go to him, yes, I will. But what am I to do?"

On that matter the spirits remained silent.

Jennet peeked around the corners before she stepped out, and followed the sound of the Frenchwoman's shrill laughter. That took her back into the dining room, where the door to the kitchens stood open. Through it she saw Greystone in a terrible state. He had been tied to a chair placed in the center of the room, and sweat gleamed on his pale face. Dozens of bleeding cuts crisscrossed his bare chest; some so deep they gaped like stretched, ghastly mouths.

He could not defend himself tied to a chair, that much was evident to her. But what monster had been torturing him?

Forcing herself to remain out of sight, Jennet watched until a smaller figure came into her view. This young woman held a bloodied boning knife in her delicate fingers. Although she had dressed as a man, she had left her brown curls loose, so they spilled artfully around her rosy-cheeked face. She didn't look aghast over Greystone's state; her expression could only be called cruel, gloating fervor.

Jennet blinked, but what she saw was not an illusion. The merry butterfly of London society, her dearest friend, the confidante she had trusted above all others, was not reeling drunk, or attempting to set Greystone free.

No, Catherine Tindall seemed very amused by her own, hideous work.

"This was only a little flirtation, William," Catherine said in French as she plied the blade along his collarbone, sending fresh blood streaking down his flesh. "We are running out of time. Now tell me what I wish to know, or I will begin to truly enjoy myself. I like to work my way from the ballocks to the brow, so you'll see everything I do until I cut out your eyes."

"Go to the devil," Greystone said in the same language, his tone taunting.

Jennet clamped down on her outrage, and braced herself against the dining room wall as she quickly thought of a dozen ways she might rescue her lover. Her gaze kept straying to an open bottle of wine that had been left on the sideboard next to her. She recalled the state Catherine had pretended to be in just before she had escorted her to the carriage, and then knew what she would do. She then closed her eyes for a moment, and silently beseeched all the souls desiring vengeance within Dredthorne Hall to come to her.

Be with me now, please. Help me to defeat her, and save my love.

The air around her grew chilly as Jennet picked up the bottle and tipped it toward herself, dribbling the wine down her front. She drank from it, just enough to scent her breath, and gripped the bottle in her fist. Rumpling her hair so that it appeared badly disordered, she staggered and collided with the door between the rooms before she burst into the kitchens.

"Catherine, is that you?" she called out in a slurred voice, and stumbled a little as she gave her a foolish grin. "You came back, and changed your costume. How original." She looked down at herself. "Oh, so did I." She frowned and swayed on her feet. "When did that happen?"

Catherine quickly stepped in front of Greystone to block him from her view. "I could not leave you here without a carriage to take you home, my dear."

"You are the very best of friends." Jennet needed to get closer, but she was not sure she had convinced the other woman. She took a drink from the bottle, and let her gaze wander around the room.

"I thought I heard Liam swearing in here. Or perhaps it was someone else. I cannot recall."

"Jennet, get the hell out of here," Greystone grated.

"No, it was him." She crooked her finger at Catherine, bending forward to say in an overloud whisper, "I remember now. He took my gown and made me wear his shirt. And between that, he ruined me again. Not like the first time. I am very, very ruined."

"Surely not," the other woman said, looking bored, and still keeping her distance.

"I assure you. Ruined forever." She held up her hand and smacked her own cheek with the back of it. "Ouch. I am so ruined I must go to a convent and become a nun. Only I am not Catholic." She peered at her former friend. "Does that matter?"

Catherine made an exasperated sound. "Generally speaking, yes."

"Pity." She managed to produce a small belch. "Oops. I hope I will not be sick." She turned around and looked all around her before regarding Catherine again. "Will you help me up to the retiring room? I cannot recall where it is. Or the door. What did you do with the door?"

"Of course." The other woman came to put her shoulder under Jennet's arm to support her. "Come, let me–"

Jennet used the wine bottle like a club to knock the blade from her hand, and then reversed the swing, striking Catherine with it squarely on the chin. The other woman flew back into the work table before she pitched forward in front of Greystone and landed on her face with a painful-sounding thud.

"It seems that I am the better actress," Jennet said as the other woman tried to rise, and kicked her in the head. She held the wine bottle ready to deal her another blow, but Catherine collapsed and stopped moving. "I cannot believe this. All this time you have pretended to be my friend while you have been spying for the French? You evil, conniving, deceitful, hateful, guttersnipe of a traitor."

"Have you taken leave of your senses?" Greystone demanded as she picked up the bloody blade and hurried over to him.

"Would you blame me if I had, after all I

have endured?" she demanded as she went around to saw through the rope binding him. When he tried pulling at his bonds she said, "Hold still. In my present mood I may pick up where Miss Tindall left off, and do far more damage to your person."

He eyed Catherine. "Indeed."

As soon as she had freed him Greystone jolted out of the chair and yanked her into his arms, holding her so tightly her ribs creaked. "You are mad. Utterly, completely, entirely mad."

"In regard to you, yes, I am." She pulled back and glanced down. "I did not kill her, which I think is a pity. She must be taken to the magistrate along with that book you left in my stays." She glared at him. "You do remember that, just before you throttled me until I swooned."

"I must take her and the book to London tonight." He picked up the rope she had cut through and expertly tied Catherine's wrists behind her back. "First I must deal with the other three agents. Did you see them?"

At that moment a man with his head wrapped in his scarf hurried in from the staircase tower landing. In his hand he held a length of blood-stained firewood.

"No, Liam," Jennet said sharply as Greystone snatched the blade from her and started for him. "Mr. Branwen, what are you doing here?"

The vicar pulled down the scarf, which she had recognized as one she had knitted for him, and sighed. "Rescuing you, Miss Reed."

The sound of heavy footsteps thumping down the stairs made them all still.

"Outside," Greystone said as he hefted Catherine's body up under his arm. "Quickly."

CHAPTER 21

When they emerged from the staircase tower, Greystone dropped Catherine's limp form by the wood bin and regarded the vicar. "Please tell me that you brought a pistol with you, Mr. Branwen."

The vicar sniffed. "I am a man of God. I do not own a pistol." He held out the length of firewood he still held, and gave it an expert swing. "I was, however, the best batsman ever to play for the Saint Peter's Smashers in college."

Jennet took something from the coat she wore, and wordlessly offered him a pistol. He saw it was the same one he had left with her in the bed chamber.

"I was saving it so I might shoot you,"

she advised him. "Fortunately, I have changed my mind."

"The Secretary at War will appreciate your restraint." He heard the agents' voices echoing in the hall as they called for Catherine, and he pointed to a spot some yards away from the door. "If you would stand over there, look terrified, and call for help when I tell you, that will draw them out."

"You wish to ambush them, then," the vicar said.

"Yes, Mr. Branwen. We will take flanking positions beside the outer door." Even with Jeffrey's help it might go badly, but this was the best chance they had of surprising the agents. "Aim for the knees of the first to come through, and I will see to the others."

"I cannot condone murder, my lord," the vicar warned him.

"Then you have come to the wrong house tonight, sir." Greystone turned to his lady, who had not moved, but looked prepared to argue. "Jenny, please. They will be in the kitchens in another moment."

"I have been abandoned, ruined,

throttled, abandoned again, and now I am made bait. To think I once wanted to marry you." She stalked over to the spot, folding her arms as he and the vicar moved to either side of the door.

Jeffrey met his gaze with a stern look. "Remember the sixth commandment, William."

"I have been too busy keeping the fifth, sir." Yet as he said that, Greystone realized that he no longer wished to kill anyone, even Catherine Tindall, who would have happily gutted him like an eel and draped herself with his entrails. "Do you believe a man of sin can start his life over again, no matter what he has done?"

"God does," the vicar assured him. "You should talk to Him about that."

Greystone looked over at Jennet. She was terrified, he knew that, and yet the worse the situation had grown, the braver she had become. She knew all of his secrets now—save one—and still she had forgiven him, and again offered him her heart.

She saw him watching her and her exasperated expression softened. "It is almost over, I hope. You can keep the pistol. I may want your ugly rings, however."

Hope was everything he had taken from her seven years ago. Whatever became of him, he had to do right by her this time. The kitchen door banged open inside the house, and he nodded to her.

"Do not let them shoot me, Liam." In a louder voice Jennet called out, "Oh, please, someone, help me."

Her cry drew the agents out through the door a moment later. As soon as Jean-Pierre barreled out the vicar swung the firewood like a cricket bat at his knee. The impact made bone crunch and buckled the man's leg, sending him sliding across the ground. He choked on the dirt filling his face, but could not rise.

As the second agent saw him go down he turned toward Greystone and brandished a long blade. He pointed Jennet's pistol down and shot him in the foot, toppling him with a howl. A boot to the jaw knocked him out cold.

The third man stopped on the threshold, staring at his comrades and then the vicar, who stood ready with the firewood. His jaw tightened.

"You should know that this man is the Raven," Jennet told him in French, and nodded at Jeffrey Branwen. "Surrender to him immediately, or I daresay he will impale you where you stand."

Greystone almost laughed out loud as the vicar took a step forward and smiled with all of his teeth.

"I have seen him do such a thing to another, my friend," Greystone told the agent, and made a gesture toward his own buttocks. "It is perhaps the worst way to die that I know."

The Frenchman stared wide-eyed at him, and dropped the blade. Gingerly he dropped to his knees and held up his hands in surrender.

Jeffrey kicked away the blade and surveyed all three men with visible satisfaction. "I do believe I came to the right house tonight."

* * *

JENNET KNEW the vicar wanted her to

accompany him to the magistrate's house. With three French agents now tied up and stowed in his carriage, and a very narrow driver's perch, there was no room for her to ride along. They also couldn't risk leaving any of the agents behind at Dredthorne Hall.

"Baron Greystone will take me home," she said to the vicar, knowing it was the kindest of lies. "I will be safe with him."

"Very well, if you are certain." Jeffrey took hold of her hands. "You are truly a remarkable young woman, and your mother should be very proud of what you did here. And I promise you, I will never breathe a word to her about any of it."

"For which you will have my eternal gratitude, Mr. Branwen. God speed." She squeezed his hands, and then stood by the lions guarding the gate and watched as he drove off.

The short walk back to Dredthorne Hall gave Jennet some time to prepare herself for what she suspected was coming. At the entry Greystone stood waiting beside two horses. Catherine, who had been gagged and securely tied across the saddle of one horse, glowered at her. She turned her back on her former friend and regarded the man about to climb onto the second mount.

He was leaving her behind again, only this time she knew why.

"You saved my life tonight," Greystone said as she removed and handed him the coat in which she'd hidden his book. He removed his own cloak, and wrapped it around her. "More importantly, you saved countless lives by helping me capture Catherine Tully and her men, and keeping the cipher out of their hands. I do not know how to thank you, Jenny."

"You are going back to France." Somehow she wasn't surprised when he nodded. "I think I knew you would. It is a time of war, and you are soldier, like my father."

"If you are…" He stopped and turned his face away from her, as if he needed to collect himself. "If you discover that you are increasing, please write to my mother, and tell her it is my child. She will not welcome the news that I am responsible, but I believe she will help you."

"What I do if I am pregnant is not your

concern. Look at me, please." When he did she walked up to him, until she was close enough to touch him, until he could feel her breath on his face. "You think that you are abandoning me again. I tell you now that you cannot. I have loved you since the first time I saw you in church. That quiet girl with the braids dreamed of meeting you again someday, so she might have the chance to become better acquainted with you. She wrote your name in her diary, over and over, next to her own. Mrs. Jennet Gerard, wife of Mr. William Gerard. You were my every hope of happiness."

"Do not do this, Jennet," he muttered.

"I have already. I saved myself for you, Liam. I always will, and whatever you choose to do, you will never truly leave me. For you will always be in my heart." She stepped back. "Good-bye, my love."

Jennet stood and watched him mount his horse, and then gazed at his back as he rode down the drive with Catherine in tow. Only when he had disappeared from sight did she wrap herself more securely in his cloak, and turn to regard the old house.

All of the windows had gone dark now,

but they reflected the full moon as if it were dozens of lamps glowing just inside the panes. The aura of menace she had sensed before had faded now, leaving behind an old, somewhat neglected house built in a time when all things French had been admired and celebrated. Perhaps someday they would be again, and someone would properly restore the place to its former glory.

Had she managed to break the curse? Jennet would never know for sure, but she had the feeling that saving the man she loved and then letting him go would have earned the approval of even the most vengeful spirit. It was what they had not been able to do as the mistresses of Dredthorne Hall.

"Perhaps you should do the same," she told the old house Hall before she started down the drive toward the road.

The walk to Reed Park on foot took most of an hour. Mrs. Holloway, who was waiting up in her nightdress and robe, unlocked the door and let her inside.

"Mrs. Reed took Barton's horse and

rode it to the parsonage," the housekeeper told her, and related the details.

The thought of her terrified, panicking mother having the courage to go for help in the middle of the night made Jennet sigh. It also meant that as soon as Jeffrey returned home he would have to bring Margaret back to hers. The poor vicar wouldn't get much sleep tonight.

"I must wash and change before she returns with Mr. Branwen," she said as she took off Greystone's cloak, revealing the bedraggled, wine-soaked shirt. "Can I impose on you to keep watch for them?"

Mrs. Holloway nodded. "I'll warm some water for you and send it up with Debny."

Upstairs Jennet gratefully stripped out of Greystone's wine-stained shirt and her undergarments, and donned her dressing gown. When her mother's maid arrived with the steaming jug, she also offered a bottle of rose water.

"For your hair, Miss." Debny grimaced at the snarled mess hanging around Jennet's face. "I'll brush it out for you once you're dressed."

"Thank you, but since I am responsible

for this disaster, I will see to it." She hesitated before she asked, "I need to speak with Mama when she arrives, and what I have to say will be distressing to her. You may want to prepare for one of her episodes."

The maid frowned. "Mrs. Reed saddled a horse to go after you tonight, Miss, and I've never seen her stronger or more determined. She panics only when she feels helpless and can do nothing. That's when her fears prey on her thinking."

Jennet felt astonished. "I have never seen that about Mama."

Debny nodded. "You always want to calm her, Miss, as you should. But the real remedy is to give her something to do about her worries. Then she is like the tiger."

Once the maid left, Jennet attended to washing and dressing herself, and brushed out her hair, braiding it as she did every night. As she did she thought of everything she had meant to conceal from Margaret, and silently debated the wisdom of doing so. If she was with child, she would need her mother's help and support. She would also have to contact William's mother, and inform her she was to become a grandmother.

Even if there was no child, Jennet still needed to explain what had happened at Dredthorne Hall. Margaret had been right about the old house, and it would gratify her to know that for once her fears had been justified.

The vicar arrived a short time later with Jennet's mother, who looked pale and exhausted. The moment Margaret saw her she opened her arms, and caught her in a tight embrace.

"Go home, dear Mr. Branwen, and bless you for delivering my girl back to me," Margaret said. "We will forever be in your debt."

Jeffrey caught Jennet's eye, and she nodded to him. "Think nothing of it, Mrs. Reed. Miss Reed." He bowed and departed.

Mrs. Holloway took Margaret's coat, and smiled as her mistress thanked her for her efforts. Jennet thought her mother might wish to retire, and suggested the same, a notion that the older woman promptly squashed.

"You will explain to me why you remained behind at Dredthorne Hall," Margaret said, and marched her into the sitting room.

After Jennet lit the lamps, she sat down with her by the banked fire, and tried to think of how to begin.

"It was William, was it not?" her mother prompted. At her incredulous look, she added, "Debny told me last week that he had come to stay at Gerard Lodge."

"Yes, he was there." Jennet took hold of her hand. "Mama, I still love him. I wish you to know that before I tell you the rest—and after tonight, I will need you."

Margaret put her arm around her, and offered Jennet her handkerchief. Only then did she feel the tears slipping down her own cheeks.

"Take your time, my dear," her mother said gently.

It did take a great deal of time to relate all of the shocking turns the masquerade ball had taken. Jennet did not go into great detail about her intimacy with Greystone, but she did not baulk at confessing she had made love with him twice. Her voice wavered as she spoke of finding Arthur Pickering murdered, and learning that the man she loved had spent the last seven years working for the crown as a spy and an assassin. But her tone hardened as she told her mother that Catherine Tindall had been doing the same for the enemy.

Jennet did not make light of seeing Greystone being tortured, or what she had done to her former friend in order to save him from that. At last she came to the moment before she had bid him farewell, and what they had said to each other.

During that time Mrs. Holloway came in quietly with two cups of chamomile tea and some toast on a tray, and left it on the table between them. By the time Jennet finished, the first rays of dawn began to lighten the room.

"That is everything, Mama." She was almost afraid to look at Margaret. "William has gone to London with Catherine and the cipher. I expect once he has turned them over to his superiors that he will return to his duties. I am sure that I will never see him again." She met her mother's gaze. "I am sorry for many things, but not for becoming his lover. Even if there is a child, I will never regret that."

The older woman handed her the now-lukewarm tisane. "I will not condemn you for loving him, my darling. Now drink, and have some toast. It will settle your nerves."

Despite her dismal mood Jennet chuckled. "I am usually the one to say that to you."

"Mrs. Branwen did the honors tonight after I arrived all hysterics at the parsonage." Margaret sighed. "She is so kind. She made tea for me, and added a jot of brandy to it. We had ginger nuts and talked of her plans for Christmas. I will have to send a note to her after I write to Lady Greystone."

"I do not think you can tell the baroness about William's work," Jennet said. "His identity must remain secret."

"I have absolutely nothing to say to Amelia about her son," her mother assured her. "But if she is to be a grandmother, then I must renew our acquaintance. Perhaps I will invite her to spend Christmas with us. She will be lonely now that her husband is gone, and we will enjoy the company."

"By then we should know, too." Jennet put down her tea cup. "What will we do if I am increasing, Mama?"

Margaret's expression turned astonished. "Why, we will go to Scotland on an extended holiday, and find a nice cottage. Perhaps on one of the islands, for they are said to be lovely. I have always wished to visit the Isle of Skye. You will wear my wedding ring, and choose a suitable surname for a married lady who has just lost her husband in the war—not Gerard, of course. Then we will go on long walks, and eat sensibly, and wait for the child. The baby will be born in the summer, when the weather is so very fine. I daresay we should invite Lady Greystone to join us there, too, once the baby has come."

"You have it all sorted." She pressed her lips together for a moment to stop them from trembling. "And if I am not with child?"

"Then we shall still go, and tour the country, and buy many fine plaids to bring back to Reed Park." Her mother kissed her cheek. "Leave it all in my hands, my darling. Whatever comes, we will be happy."

CHAPTER 22

From Renwick Greystone rode directly to London, stopping only once to water and rest the horses. Dawn came before he reached the city, so he covered Catherine Tindall with the coat Jennet had given him. Tucking it around her concealed her form as well as her bonds, but she made furious sounds and struggled under the heavy wool.

"Be silent and still, and you may live to hate the English another day," Greystone told her. "Keep fighting, and I will finish what Jennet started at the hall."

He rode to a livery in Cheapside that did much more than hire out carriages and horses, and gave the burly stable hand who came to meet him his passcode. The station to which he reported was not his usual stop when he came to London, but as soon as he explained himself to the chief officer he was provided with fresh clothing and a carriage with an armed driver. The last he saw of Catherine was when she was marched back to one of the cells hidden behind the stalls to await transport to prison. They had kept her hands tied behind her back, but removed her gag.

She glanced back over her shoulder at him, her pretty face smeared with dirt and her eyes dull with defeat. Then she spat in his direction.

Greystone felt a curious sense of seeing his own fate, had it not been thwarted. *If not for Jennet, that would be me.*

From the station, the carriage took Greystone to Whitehall, and the Horse Guards building across from St. James's Palace. Soldiers and certain members of government were permitted into the old red brick building, which most of London regarded as a barracks and stable for the most senior Army regiments. The Secretary at War and his staff encouraged this illusion.

Guards stopped Greystone at five different checkpoints before he was permitted access to the war room, where his superiors worked tirelessly to gather and analyze the latest reports to advise Wellington and Parliament on the war effort. Today he found three older statesmen with one of the general's most trusted spymasters, a quartet wryly known among their agents as the Four Horsemen.

He wasted no time after greeting them as he placed the cipher onto the map table. "Gentlemen, Arthur Pickering died last night to protect this from French agents on English soil. I was obliged to deliver it myself. I hope it was worth his life."

The spymaster, a reedy man with little hair and flat eyes, picked up the book and skimmed through it.

"We shall see to it that it is." He glanced at the other three men, who abruptly left the room, and then regarded Greystone. "My station chief advises that you captured and brought in Ruban as well. Quite unsettling for me to learn that he is actually an Irish woman."

Reporting on what he had learned from

Catherine Tully, Greystone also recommended they collect her parents and the other three agents from the magistrate in Renwick before any of them managed to get word out of their capture.

"Yes, that will keep the French using the same cipher for some weeks yet, until one of their more intelligent generals works out that we have it." The spymaster smiled a little. "This, along with the elimination of Ruban, could very well turn the tide of the war to our favor. You are to be commended, Raven, even if I can never do so officially."

"Thank you, sir." He suppressed the sudden urge to lunge at his superior. "I should like to return to France as soon as may be arranged."

"I am afraid that Arthur Pickering did not share your opinion." The older man pocketed the cipher. "I received a report from him last week concerning your fitness for duty. For many reasons, including your inheritance of the barony, he felt this operation should be your last. I am inclined to agree."

Greystone shrugged. "I liked Pickering,

but he was just a courier. I am more than willing to continue serving."

"We do not always inform our agents as to who they work with, or what their real responsibilities are," the spymaster chided. "Arthur was my most trusted analyst, and evaluated for me the performance of all our overseas operatives."

So Arthur had had other motives for bringing him to Renwick. Greystone didn't know what to say in his defense. All he could think was what the vicar had said to him just before they had routed Catherine's men.

The spymaster took out his pocket watch to check the time. "I am due to brief the Prime Minister and the Secretary at War within the hour, so I must keep this brief. In a few days we will let it slip that Arthur Pickering was the Raven, so the French will believe they have achieved some small victory over us. We will arrange to have the merchant, Guillame Girard, die in a tragic carriage accident while traveling in Provence. Ruban will go to the gallows, and her family persuaded to talk, unless they wish to suffer the same. I expect they will hang rather than cooperate."

It took William a moment for him to gather enough breath to speak. "What am I to do, then?"

"Why, you will now retire from our service, William, and return to the life you should have had these seven years—with our gratitude, sir." The spymaster touched his shoulder. "I suggest you take some time for yourself. The transition will be made easier that way. Perhaps a long holiday in the country will help."

Could it be this simple? "Sir, what am I permitted to tell my family?"

"You may tell everything to those you trust to keep it to themselves. Your mother, certainly. No harm can come from it now." The older man grinned. "After all, the Raven is dead. Long live Baron Greystone."

THE ANCIENT BUTLER who opened the door to the London house looked down his nose at Greystone. Since he was a head shorter, that required a remarkable arrangement of his neck and head. But John Morris had a lifetime of service to the Gerards, as well as the baron's chilly example, which had helped perfect his disdainful posturing.

"Her ladyship is not receiving," the old man told him in a tight, disapproving tone. He didn't have to add 'you, ever' to the end of that statement.

"Get out of my way, Morris, or I will move you." Greystone looked down at the cane the butler had butted against his belly. He felt a flicker of admiration for the old man, who he could probably snap in half. "Permit me inside, and it will be the last time I darken these premises. I swear it."

Morris's nostrils flared, but he didn't move out of the way.

"I have spent seven years dealing with the mess my father made of my life." He was coming perilously close to shouting, but he didn't care. "I was never allowed to tell my mother a word about it. Father forbid that, and he never told her. Today I have been released from my duties to the crown, and from my promises to him. By God, she will know the truth now, if I must stand out in the street and shout it at her window."

"It is all right, Morris," a tired voice said from the hall behind him.

As soon as the butler lowered his cane and stepped inside Greystone crossed the threshold, and saw his mother standing outside her morning room. She wore lavender for half-mourning, her gown a simple but elegant style. Although her shoulders had grown slightly stooped, and her hair had gone completely silver, she had changed little over the last year. Yet in her eyes was the same melancholy he had seen at his father's funeral.

Suddenly Greystone didn't know what he would say to her. "Thank you for seeing me, my lady."

"Morris, please advise the Cook that we will want coffee, not tea." The baroness retreated into her morning room.

Much of the interior of his parents' home had changed since his last visit; he could see his mother had softened the starkness his father had preferred with pleasant colors and more comfortable furnishings. In the morning room she had a large standing embroidery hoop by her chair, on which she had stitched a panel with flowers and birds. He admired her handiwork for a moment before he went to sit down across from her.

He waited until a maid brought the ordered coffee and left before he said, "You told me to remember my choice. I wish you to know that I never made that choice. Father took that from me."

His mother poured a cup for him and added cream but no sugar, just as he had always preferred it. "You blame my husband for your behavior, then. How commonplace of you. I suppose I am to blame as well for your heartlessness."

"You are not, my lady," Morris said from the doorway. The old man regarded Greystone. "Do not do this thing, sir. If you tell her, it will crush her."

"What are you talking about?" Lady Greystone looked astonished. "Morris?"

Before he had become the baroness's butler, Greystone recalled, Morris had been his father's valet.

"Do you have any notion of what it has done to me?" he asked the old man, who hung his head and then hobbled off. He turned to face his mother. "I did not choose to abandon Jennet Reed seven years ago. Father commanded me to."

The baroness went still. "Why in Heaven's name would he do such a thing?"

* * *

THE DAY before his wedding William Gerard spent the morning finishing the final fitting for his new dark blue cut away jacket, which had required a slight adjustment to accommodate his broad shoulders. It matched his skin-tight knee breeches, which were all the fashion now, and made the spotless white muslin of his shirt look as if it had been woven of swan's down. His choice of an apricot-colored silk cravat and a scarlet waist coat had met with supreme disapproval from the tailor in London, but he didn't care. He wanted to make his lady smile when she saw him waiting for her at the altar.

He returned to Gerard Lodge, where the housekeeper informed him that his mother had gone to the village church to check the flower arrangements.

"The baron has returned from London,

Mr. William," she added. "He bade me ask you to attend him as soon as you arrived. He's reading in his book room."

William went to the back of the house, where his father kept a large room filled with the books that he collected during his travels. Most were in French, but the baron seemed indifferent to how unpatriotic his selections could be viewed. He often spoke in the same language sometimes without thinking.

"Welcome home, Father," he said as he came in, and then stopped when he saw how pale and gaunt the baron appeared. He also reclined on a chaise, something he had never seen him do. "Never tell me that you are unwell. I am to be married tomorrow." When his father simply looked up at him, he said, "I will send for Dr. Mallory at once."

"Do not bother. He cannot help me." Charles Gerard set aside the book he had been reading, and sat up. "Come here to me, boy. We have much to discuss before your mother returns."

William had never been openly affectionate with the baron, who discouraged such emotional demonstrations, but he had always respected his father. Slowly he came to sit beside him on the chaise. "What is it? Mother said that you had a minor cold."

"It seemed so, at first, and then I felt pains in my chest. I went to see my physician in London before I left the city." The baron's voice had grown ragged, and he cleared his throat several times before he said, "He found fluid in my lungs, and an alteration in the function of my heart. These can be treated, and with care I may live several more years, but there is no cure."

His father had always seemed indestructible to William, and the thought of him dying had never entered his thoughts.

"Surely we must obtain another opinion," he said. "Perhaps on the continent. They say the Swiss doctors are some of the finest in the world."

Charles shook his head. "This is the same malady that killed my grandfather. As a boy I watched his decline. It began as my own did, with weakness in the limbs, and breathlessness after even the slightest exertion. He became bed-ridden after a year. I expect the same will happen to me."

"Then we will look after you, mother and I," William assured him. "You will want for nothing, I promise you."

"I never expected that it would come over me so quickly," his father said, almost as if he were talking to himself now. "My grandfather was ten years my senior when he took ill. I should have noticed the signs earlier, but this damned war…"

Now William felt confused. "What has the war to do with your condition?"

The baron stared at him for a long moment. "It is like gazing into a mirror, when I look upon you. Even our voices are indistinguishable. I wish you to know that is what led to my resolve. I do not wish to encumber you with my burdens, but it seems I must."

"Anything, Father." William took hold of his hand. "Tell me what I can do."

* * *

ONCE GREYSTONE FINISHED RELATING the

details of that conversation, and everything that had followed it, he rose and went to the window to look out on the street. The elegant lords and ladies passing by in their barouches and curricles appeared happy to be out driving around town. Soon they would begin making their afternoon calls, and then attend whatever entertainments they had arranged for the evening.

Lady Greystone came to stand beside him, and watched for a moment before she said, "Tell me what I can do."

That she had unconsciously repeated his own words to the baron made him smile a little. "Forgive me. Father swore me to secrecy for as long as I served as the Raven. If you would, please advise Morris that I have your permission to come and call on you now. I have missed you so much, and I think I will have great need of your wisdom now."

Her eyes shimmered as she looked up at him. "I loved your father, but dear God. I could kill him for what he has done to you."

"Too late, Mama," he said gently.

With a sob his mother embraced him, and he led her back over to the settee and held her as she wept. Once she had regained control of herself she told him that he must return home and live with her now, so they might make up for all the years they had spent apart.

"I have one more confession to make," Greystone admitted. "I must go back to Renwick and see Jennet."

The baroness rose and went to her writing desk, where she took a small box from a drawer and brought it to him. "You will offer this to Miss Reed."

He took the box and held it in his hands. "She will throw it back in my face."

"Then you will offer it again, and again, until the lady changes her mind about you." His mother smiled. "I expect that will take some time. I will pack up the household and move into Gerard Lodge. You will need a place to sleep, and I do not wish to be far from you again."

He nodded, and then recalled what Morris had said. "Have I crushed you, Mother? I know how devoted you were to him."

Lady Greystone gave him an impatient look. "You ask me that, after what he did to you? I have never been so angry with your father in my life. I daresay I could dig up his grave and set fire to his bones." She let out a breath. "It does explain, however, his last words to me. He asked me to beg your forgiveness for the burden he had given to you. I never understood that until now."

"Do not dig his grave." He kissed her brow. "Pack up the house and go to Gerard Lodge. I will see you there tomorrow."

$\mathcal{A}$ week after the masquerade at Dredthorne, Jennet returned from attending to some errands in the village to find her mother anxiously awaiting her.

"Oh, you are alive, my dear, thank Heavens." Margaret embraced her as if she had returned from a year-long absence. "When Debny told me you had left, I thought I might swoon with terror." She stepped back and held up her hands. "No, I am not doing this again. I knew you would be fine. I must rid myself of these pointless anxieties."

Jennet drew back and smiled. "I went only to fetch that lace you ordered last month, and some supplies for Mrs. Holloway."

She had also casually inquired if Greystone had by chance returned to Gerard Lodge, but all she learned was that he remained in London. That meant he had probably already left for France.

"I do not like it when you leave me," Margaret said. "But I am determined to improve on myself, and learn to trust you will come back to me."

"I always will." She stroked her mother's back. "All of the danger is over now, Mama."

"I try not to think on poor Mr. Pickering and his men, snatched so cruelly from life," her mother said as she walked from one window to the next to peer out at the gardeners. "And the Tindalls, whom we considered very good friends, exposed as French spies and carted off to the gaol. Try as I will, I cannot help but to envision what new terrors will befall us next. Does that monster Bonaparte plot to invade Renwick some night soon, and murder us all in our beds?"

"Wellington will never allow that, Mama," Jennet told Margaret as she poured a cup of chamomile tea for her. "Come and sit down. You will wear out the rugs if you keep pacing so. Besides, I asked Cook to make fairy cakes for your tea."

Her mother stopped in her tracks. "The little ones with the butter icing?"

"The very same," she assured her, holding out the tea.

The treat lured Margaret to her favorite spot by the hearth, where she sat and nibbled while Jennet related the least alarming news from the village. That included the long-awaited engagement of Prudence Hardiwick.

"Lady Hardiwick must be none too pleased that her daughter has accepted Peter Mason," Margaret said. "His means are quite modest, and he looks after his widowed sister."

"Her ladyship told me herself while I was in the haberdasher's shop." Jennet had felt pleased to hear it as well, for it proved Prudence had taken her reading to heart. "She seems more relieved than annoyed, and plans an early spring wedding."

"As naughty as Prudence can be? I

should obtain a special license and have them to the church by week's end." Her mother dabbed at her lips with a napkin. "Oh, these cakes are delightful. You always know how to cheer me, my dear."

That she did, Jennet thought, feeling a little depressed now. She had nothing to regret, of course, and felt quite capable of managing anything after surviving that night at Dredthorne Hall. In the weeks to come she would learn if there would be a child, and if so she and Margaret would act on the plans they had made. Doubtless they could find a pleasant cottage in a small Scottish town where she could spend her confinement. Having her mother with her would be a great comfort when the baby came.

"I think I will take a turn out of doors before it grows too cold," Jennet said, refilling her mother's tea cup before she rose. "I will return in half an hour."

"Please stay to the gardens, where I can see you," Margaret asked, and then grimaced. "I know I am being ridiculous again, but it comforts me to keep you in my sight."

"You have always kept me safe, Mama." Jennet bent to kiss her mother's brow. "There is nothing silly about that."

Outside clouds blanketed the November skies, and the bite of the breeze made Jennet wrap her cloak more tightly around her. She walked out from the terrace to where she might sit by the fountain. But she stopped in her tracks when she saw the man who waited there, his wind-swept hair now gleaming black, with only a few strands of silver. He regarded her with his hooded green eyes, beneath which lay the dark smudges left by what she assumed had been several sleepless nights.

Good, then he had suffered as much as she, Jennet thought, and not gone to France. Perhaps she was the love of his life, then. He was certainly hers.

"You stole my cloak," Greystone said as he watched her approach.

She glanced down at herself. "You traded it for a coat before you rode off with Catherine to London. It is now my cloak."

"I have come for you," he told her. "Not the damned cloak."

"Whatever for?" Her gaze went to his

hands, in which he held a small ring box, and she skittered backward. "Oh, no. Not again. We have already done this once, sir, and it ended very badly for me. Go back to France. You seem much happier when you are killing people."

Greystone gave her an exasperated look. "My superiors have let it slip that Pickering was the Raven. Guillame Girard, the merchant, has died in France. I am to return to a private life as a gentleman. You are my wife now in everything but name. For God's sake, Jenny, put me out of my misery and marry me."

Jennet knew there was more to it than that, and sat down beside him. "You still have secrets. I can see them in your eyes."

"I came to tell you the last of them," Greystone said. "And then I meant to propose."

"You've done one," she said. "Now the other."

"My father was the Raven," he said, and looked out at the horizon. "He created Guillame Girard and served the crown as an assassin for many years. It was why he was away from home so often, but not even my mother knew. Seven years ago, Father began to have pains in his chest and difficulty breathing. The doctors told him that his heart and lungs were failing, and he could no longer exert himself as he had. That was when he told me the truth, because he needed me to be the Raven."

A terrible certainty filled her. "Your father asked you to take his place."

He nodded. "You remember that we looked enough alike to be twin brothers. My grandmother was half French, and my mother saw to it that I could speak the language like a native. Father's spymaster and his people trained me to do the rest."

She gripped the edge of the fountain's basin. "You could not refuse him?"

"Father made it clear what would happen if Guillame Girard suddenly disappeared without explanation," he admitted. "Every agent who had worked with him would have been arrested and interrogated. Bonaparte's Minister of Police is a merciless brute. Most would have been tortured to death, leaving destitute their wives and children."

"You really had no choice." Jennet

shuddered. "If you had explained this to me seven years ago, I would have called off the wedding." And she would have waited for him, not that she would tell him that.

Greystone took hold of her hand. "I first learned of my father's work as an assassin on the day before we were to be married. He told me that I would have to leave for France by the week's end. I could not marry you, or even tell you why I had to go. Father insisted that everyone believe that I had changed my mind and run."

Jennet could not imagine the torment he must have felt. "Have you told the baroness the truth?"

"I did before I came here, but only because we were both in London." He rubbed his thumb across her palm. "She is traveling to Gerard Lodge today."

Jennet looked down as she felt him slip a ring onto her finger. A square-cut diamond twinkled up at her. "You are very quick, my lord. I have not yet given you my answer."

"I may have given you my child," Greystone told her very sternly. "If not, I will try very hard to remedy that every night henceforth." He touched her cheek. "Come to Scotland with me now, Jenny. We can be married by the morning, and return to Renwick as we should always have been: husband and wife."

"Well, I do like your mother and Gerard Lodge." She studied her new ring. "You are a very wealthy peer of the realm. Should anyone threaten me, you would prove an adequate bodyguard. Rose Abernathy will be absolutely livid. Hmm."

"I will make an offer for Dredthorne Hall, if you wish." He chuckled as she swatted him. "It is the place where we fell in love again."

"I hated you," Jennet confessed. "I cursed you, and burned all of your notes and cards and the flowers I had pressed. I never spoke your name, and tried every day to forget you. And I never stopped loving you. Not for a moment."

He brought her hand to his lips. "Nor I you."

Jennet heard the door to the terrace opening, and looked up to see Margaret rushing straight for them.

"All is well, Mama," she said quickly as she and Greystone got to their feet. "Ah, you remember Liam?"

"I know precisely who he is. Well, sir, you have considerable nerve to show your face on my property." Margaret stopped in front of them and stared at Jennet's hand. "Just a moment. William, did you put that ring on my daughter's finger?"

"I did, ma'am." Greystone bowed, but as he came back up the older woman balled up her fist and punched him in the nose.

Jennet's jaw dropped. "Mama."

Margaret shook her hand. "You have my blessing, sir. Please, do stay and dine with us. We should begin planning the wedding at once." She smiled at him. "And if you leave my daughter standing alone in a church again, or in any way disgrace her or our family name, I will hunt you down and shoot you dead myself."

Greystone bowed again, and then watched as her mother marched back into the house. "I think we are not eloping, Jenny," he said as he put his arm around her.

"I daresay." She leaned against him. "She still has Father's pistols."

THE END

303

More Books by Hazel Hunter

DEDICATION

For Mr. H.

9 781950 575183